MURDER O
ALLEY

MURDER ON TIN PAN ALLEY

THE SECOND BOBBIE FLYNN MYSTERY

JACK MURRAY

Books by Jack Murray

Kit Aston Mysteries.
The Affair of the Christmas Card Killer
The Chess Board Murders.
The Phantom Museum
The Frisco Falcon
The Medium Murders
The Bluebeard Club
The Tangier Tajine
The Empire Theatre Murders
The Newmarket Murders
The New Year's Eve Murders
The French Diplomat Affair (novella)
Haymaker's Last Fight (novelette)

DI Jellicoe Mysteries
A Time to Kill
The Bus Stop
Trio
Dolce Vita Murders

Agatha Aston Mysteries
Black-Eyed Nick
The Witchfinder General Murders
The Christmas Murder Mystery
The Siegfried Slayer (Oct 2023)

Danny Shaw / Manfred Brehme WWII Series
The Shadow of War
Crusader
El Alamein

The Bobbie Flynn Mysteries
A Little Miss Taken
Murder on Tin Pan Alley
Murder at the Metropolitan

Copyright © 2024 by Jack Murray

All rights reserved. No part of this publication may be reproduced, distributed, or transmitted in any form or by any means, including photocopying, recording, or other electronic or mechanical methods, without the prior written permission of the publisher, except in the case of brief quotations embodied in critical reviews and certain other non-commercial uses permitted by copyright law. For permission requests, write to the publisher, addressed 'Attention: Permissions Coordinator,' at the address below.

Jackmurray99@hotmail.com

This is a work of fiction. Names, characters, businesses, places, events, locales, and incidents are either the products of the author's imagination or used in a fictitious manner. Any resemblance to actual persons, living or dead, or actual events is purely coincidental.

Cover by Jack Murray

ISBN: 9798323784585
Imprint: Independently published

For my dad and mum who introduced me to this wonderful music.

This is for you…

1

Early morning, W43rd Street, New York: 21st January 1922

Few people go to work each morning singing a happy song. Probably they are counting down to that wonderful day when retirement beckons bringing with it endless days of gadding about, gardening or golf.

Detective Sean Nolan was neither a gardener nor a golfer and retirement was at least thirty years away. For the time being, the most he could look forward to was going into work and not having to view a dead body first thing in the morning.

Today was not going to be one of those days.

Nolan stared down at the corpse lying on the bed of the apartment. He presumed the man was dead. There was a pillow over his head that had been used to muffle the sound of a gunshot. He hadn't, yet, looked underneath the pillow, but the quantity of blood, staining both the destroyed pillow and the bedsheets, did not augur well for the body on the bed.

Beside him was his partner, Detective Tim Yeats. They were a contrasting pair. Nolan was six feet tall, broad shouldered and slender. Yeats was as tall as Nolan and just as wide. Nolan was quiet, thoughtful and serious. Yeats was loud, impulsive and Nolan's best friend on the force.

Nolan looked around the dingy, one bedroom apartment and wondered how anyone could live in such a tiny and less-than-luxurious space. The wallpaper was torn, revealing cracks and holes in the wall. He didn't envy anyone that would have to take fingerprints in this room. It had the minimum of furniture: a bed, a set of drawers with a mirror, a chair upon which were draped coats and trousers. The only other piece of furniture in the room was an upright piano, with half a dozen books of sheet music perched precariously on the music stand.

With something approaching relief, Nolan turned his attention to the murder weapon, lying beside the body of the dead man. It was an army service revolver. The question of how the dead man could have been killed by such a weapon possibly had its answer on the wall. There was a photograph of a group of soldiers.

Nolan's eyes returned to the body. Steeling himself, he took away the pillow. The man was dead. No doubt about it. The bullet hole in the temple was a pretty big clue, no matter how you looked at it.

Nolan estimated that he was around twenty-five to thirty. His body was slender with dark hair, stained red by the gunshot. A medical examiner would be along soon who would confirm if this were the cause, together with the time of death. While he had only been a detective for a couple of years, Nolan guessed the man had been dead for less than three hours based on the level of rigor that had set in. This would put the time of death at around five in the morning, or soon after.

Yeats was on his knees by a chair and rifling through the pockets of the trousers that had been set on it. It was a gruesome business and the big detective made quick work of the task. The man's clothes were folded neatly.

Army-style.

'Nothing,' said Yeats, getting to his feet.

Outside in the corridor they heard the sound of the man's neighbours inquiring from the uniformed policeman at the door what was happening. Nolan went to the door and opened it slightly. He spoke to the patrol man there.

'Take a statement, will you. Find out as much as you can about this guy and who visited him regularly, and last night in particular. And find the superintendent of the building. Who came in last night? Who left this morning? I want names.'

'Yes sir,' said the patrol man. The door closed as the policeman said to the man, 'Okay, bud, tell me about this guy.'

Nolan took in the room from the doorway. It was the sort of apartment that you could search in a matter of minutes. Nolan shook his head and wondered what sort of a man would choose to live here and then he stopped himself. Life did not present choices for everyone. Only a fortunate few could look life in the eye and dictate terms.

Nolan was not sure if he qualified completely on this score. He was twenty-six, still living with his mother and a cat. He could probably afford to live in his own place, but his pay as a detective meant he would be living on dog food. Not much choice there. There wasn't much choice when Uncle Sam had pointed to him and said, "I want you for the U.S. Army" in 1917. Him and a few others in his neighbourhood had gone over. Few came back. No, choices were for a select few. The rest of us, he mused, get carried along by the tide. Most learn to swim, but always with the current.

The dead man was ex-army. The photograph of him and his buddies was just like one Nolan had in his bedroom, stuck inside the rim of the mirror. Nolan wondered how many had survived. There were five men in the picture. Probably they would have to find out who they were, who'd made it back, who hadn't. He would wait until the fingerprints had been taken before removing the photograph from the frame. He hoped there were names on the back. Did one of them have a motive to do this?

Someone had a motive, clearly. The blood around the dead man's head suggested it was a pretty big one. It took a lot of anger to do what had been done to this dead man. A lot of anger indeed. Or fear.

There were another couple of photographs. One with the dead man and another man who looked very like him, only older. The last photograph was of an older woman. Nolan guessed this was his mother. He wondered if she was still alive. It might be better if she wasn't. This would be the very worst news for any parent,

'So, what do you think, Holmes?' asked Yeats, with a grin.

Holmes was a pet name for Nolan from Yeats. A few other guys at the precinct had started to call him this too. It was affectionate rather than pointed. Nolan was popular, he was also smart and the men rated him. More importantly, his success rate was high.

Nolan's lips twitched a little, but he resisted a smile. The gallows humour most cops shared, was a self-defence against the sight and sound of life's very harshest reality. Nolan was not above using such humour himself, but he was not always entirely comfortable indulging in it.

The dead man, like the detective, had made it through the War, only to have his life ended prematurely in a low rent room. He felt sad for the man and wondered if there would be anyone to grieve him.

There was a knock on the door.

'Come in,' said Nolan.

The door opened, it was the uniformed policeman that Nolan had spoken to earlier, 'Mr Laszlo is back.' Laszlo was the superintendent of the building. 'He's the one who found the body,' explained the patrol man.

Nolan nodded and went to the door. He stood blocking the view of the apartment from Laszlo and the neighbour.

'What have you got?' asked Nolan.

Laszlo handed him a few documents, including a rental agreement and some unopened mail. The name on the envelope was George Rankin. Nolan fixed his eyes on the tenement manager.

'Rankin here long?' he asked.

'Nearly a year. Usually paid on time. Maybe late sometimes but not often. Nice enough guy in small doses. Chatty. Didn't know when to stop sometimes.'

'You said he was a song plugger to one of the men earlier,' prompted Nolan.

'That's what he said. He was always singing songs on the piano.'

Song plugger.

Well, it was a job. Nolan knew little about what it entailed but suspected that there was less to it than met the name. A guy who plugged songs. Seemed simple enough. Nolan supposed it was like a door-to-door Bible salesman, only for songs. Somebody had to do it.

'Yeah, he played the piano real good too.'

Nolan's gaze switched, involuntarily, down to the bloodied face of the man who had played it, possibly the night before.

'I guess not everyone thought so,' said Nolan, sadly. He went out of the room and followed Laszlo down the stairs to his office.

Ferenc Laszlo was the superintendent of the building. He was as tall as Nolan and as broad as Yeats. Not someone you would go out of your way to mess around. His office, by the entrance of the building, was large enough to accommodate someone from Lilliput, but had not been designed with someone of Laszlo's dimensions in mind. He smiled when he saw Nolan's eyes scan the office before resting on him.

'Not very big, no?'

The accent was Hungarian, a country he had left only eight years before. His desire to avoid fighting in the upcoming war was matched only by a curiosity about the new world. With or without a war, Laszlo would have made the journey west.

'Coffee?' asked the Hungarian holding up a dirty cup. Nolan declined, politely.

'Have you a list of people or tradesmen who entered the building this morning?' asked Nolan. He was handed a list by way of reply. There were three names on it. Nolan pointed to the first man, Glen Fisher, who had come to the building at six thirty in the morning.

'Glen Fisher was here to fix pipes. I know him. Comes many times.'

Next on the list was Al Eklund. He came just before seven.

'Apartment 201 has problem with electricity.'

'You know him?'

'Yes, I know very well,' said Laszlo. Then added, 'He's sixty-five.'

Nolan wasn't sure if his age would necessarily disqualify him from murder, but he quite liked the big Hungarian, who combined good humour with a sense of sadness at what had happened, not an easy manner to carry off.

The final name on the list was a woman, named Lucy Deng. She had arrived at the same time as Eklund.

'Cleaner. Mops stairs, you know, the usual.'

Nolan nodded. Then he fixed his eyes on Laszlo, 'You're sure no one else could have come in or left between six and when we came?'

'No. I was here. If I no see them then Al or Lucy would have. Simple,' said Laszlo.

This seemed clear and the Hungarian was nothing if not credible. Which did not preclude him from being a suspect for the killing.

'What was Mr Rankin like? Did he have many visitors?'

The superintendent's face became sad and he shook his head.

'Good guy. No problem. Not many visitors. Maybe a girl sometimes. It's sad. Who do this?'

Who indeed, thought Nolan. It was going to be his job to find out. He sighed and nodded a thanks to the big Hungarian. Something about this killing felt like it was going to be one of those difficult investigations. There was no obvious motive and the killer seemed like a ghost.

Then again, they usually all started out this way. The one thing he had to remember was that someone, somewhere, needed George Rankin to be dead and either they or someone they had employed, had killed him. This meant there was a motive and someone had both the opportunity and the means to carry out the murder.

2

Greenwich Village, New York: 21st January 1922

The smell of freshly baked bread wafted in from the kitchen, accompanied by several words of Spanish that were unlikely to grace a children's book any time soon. The creator of the intoxicating aroma and the owner of the foul mouth were one and the same person: a diminutive septuagenarian Spaniard by the name of Mrs Garcia. She was the housekeeper for the Flynns and had been so for the past twenty years, since before Bobbie Flynn could walk.

Thanks to Mrs Garcia, Bobbie could both converse and swear in Spanish with equal facility. The latter was known only unto Mrs Garcia and she did not approve although, equally, she could hardly complain as she was the source of Bobbie's erudition. If ever Bobbie got into a knife fight in Mexico City, Mrs Garcia's birthplace, then she probably would not survive but, at least, her attacker would be given to understand, in almost explicit terms, just what a so-and-so he was.

Inspector Flynn, Bobbie's father, closed his eyes and took in the smell of the bread. It was Sunday morning and he was off duty. He had nothing planned that day which suited him just fine. The only thing in his diary at that moment was eating the breakfast that was tantalising his olfactory sense. He resisted the temptation to shout to Mrs Garcia to get a move on as he knew this would result in Bobbie collapsing with laughter and the bread being hurled violently at his head. Perhaps he would try and grab nine holes later in the day. He'd see what the weather was like.

Mrs Garcia ruled this roost with a sharp tongue. Flynn knew his place and stuck to it like a sentry on night duty. Moments later, the little woman appeared from the kitchen, hidden behind a tray with a large loaf of bread, still steaming hot. She placed it on the table and allowed her acolytes to drink in the atmosphere surrounding her creation.

Then she disappeared before returning a few moments later with two plates containing eggs, bacon and many other items of food for a generation brought up blissfully free of finger-wagging healthy eating fanatics.

'Smells good Mrs Garcia,' said Bobbie.

'Bet your butt it does, Red,' said Mrs Garcia. Like many people, not including Flynn or his late wife, Nancy, Bobbie was known as Red, by most people who knew her on account of her auburn hair, rather than any pointed observation to a volatility of temperament.

Flynn said nothing, as he had already torn into the breakfast with gusto. He was not one for conversation while there was food to be eaten. This brought a roll of the eyes from the two women.

'So, when is the brat coming?' asked Mrs Garcia. 'I thought she would be here by now.'

'Later this morning,' answered Bobbie, between mouthfuls. 'And she's not a brat. Give her a chance.'

'We'll see about that,' responded Mrs Garcia, sceptically. 'Anyone from Hell's Kitchen is a brat in my book.'

'As opposed to Spanish Harlem?' interjected Flynn.

'We're uptown, at least,' pointed out the little Mexican woman primly.

The brat in question was Violet Scott who had been, briefly, adopted by the Belmont family, before Bobbie had uncovered the fact that they were implicated in murder and kidnapping. Such inclinations are, unsurprisingly, frowned upon by orphanages when they are seeking foster parents, even for the children of Hell's Kitchen. Violet's father was still alive, but his circumstances were considered so degraded as to represent a possible danger to the life of the child. Violet had been returned to the Roman Catholic Orphan Asylum, where she had expected to spend the next few years of her life.

Fate had other plans. These took the shape of Bobbie Flynn, the twenty-one-year-old daughter of a long-suffering, senior police detective who had a difficult enough life as it was without a journalist daughter with one eye on the crime beat and another fixed on being a foster parent to a precocious eleven-year-old girl.

Bobbie's case to her father had run something along the lines of "it's not like we haven't the room or the money". Both were unarguable, which is probably why Bobbie chose this territory to base her fight. Like most chaps, whose desire for an easy life is often completely thwarted by a female species who detest seeing them loafing around, Flynn had to submit rather than face years of silently deafening opprobrium from his daughter.

'Is she coming here?' asked Mrs Garcia.

'No, daddy and I are taking her to a show on Broadway.'

Flynn's eyes widened. He'd forgotten about the show. So much for the nine holes. He sighed briefly and then felt the bread melt on his tongue. Life could be harder than this, he decided. Aware of Mrs Garcia's eyes on him, Flynn pointedly ignored her by picking up the newspaper that had been delivered, effectively hiding him from the female gaze as men have done for eons.

'Coward,' said Mrs Garcia, which provoked a grin from Bobbie and rumble from Flynn.

'Haven't you fired her yet?' growled Flynn broadly in the direction of Bobbie.

Bobbie ignored her father and added for the benefit of Mrs Garcia, 'We're taking her to a matinee of the "*Music Box Revue*" and then we'll have an early dinner. We'll take her back to the orphanage after that.'

'Dinner?' asked Mrs Garcia. 'So, you don't want me to make anything for tonight?'

'No, I'll be back later,' said Flynn, flicking the newspaper to one side. The paper was the *New York American*, which Bobbie worked on. She wrote obituaries for both the morning and evening versions of the paper. Her real desire was to be a crime reporter, but she was facing a combination of resistance, chap in origin, against such a move. Sadly, this opposition was rather powerful and twofold: both her father and the ruthless newspaper editor, Thornton Kent, were proving insurmountable obstacles to her ambition.

'You would,' said Mrs Garcia, which could have meant anything and was ignored by the target of her barb.

'What are you planning to do anyway?' asked Flynn, lowering the paper now that the coast was clear of their opinionated Mexican housekeeper.

'I have a surprise for her,' said Bobbie, and related what she had set up for a young girl who had recently experienced the trauma of kidnap and losing her foster parents.

'You would,' said Flynn, taking a leaf from their housekeeper's book, before returning to his newspaper.

While Bobbie and her father made their way to the Bronx to meet with Violet, the child in question was having a light lunch. Her day had begun quite a bit earlier, at seven, with mass. Following this, she had had breakfast and then gone to the library to read the newspaper and then a book. After this, she had joined some of the other girls and played indoors as the weather was a winning combination of wind and rain.

This was the third time Bobbie and Flynn had taken her out for the day. Bobbie was intent on fostering Violet or, at least, making her a ward. With each day out, Violet's reserve was diminishing. While she liked Bobbie, it was clear to her that Flynn was more sceptical about Bobbie's intentions.

In many ways, Violet could not blame the old detective. She was unsure too. The high, of being adopted by the Belmonts, had been replaced by the low of realisation that it had all been a sham, part of a wider plan to make money from the family of the girl she had befriended. Still, a day out to the theatre was not to be sniffed at. Especially with Bobbie, who she certainly did like.

Violet's favourite nun was Sister Assumpta. She had befriended the nun when she had first been resident at the orphanage, a few years earlier. Their friendship had resumed upon her return. This time around, Violet had vowed she would stay with the old nun who, at least, had always been loyal and caring towards her. Outsiders were not to be trusted. Her view on this was being shaken, by contact with Bobbie. As she saw the nun come towards her, she felt the stab of disloyalty as she was looking forward to seeing the Flynns, even the father.

Her relationship with the father was an odd one. He was cranky and sharp with her in equal measure. As she had nothing tying her to him, she was cranky and sharp with him too. She quite enjoyed the freedom to give the old detective a hard time. She felt, intuitively, he enjoyed it too, as he never seemed to take offence or tell her off for being naughty.

'Your friends are here,' announced Sister Assumpta with a smile. If it were in the gift of the old nun, she would have handed over Violet to the odd pair immediately. She liked them both and, more importantly, she trusted them. Any thoughts that she would miss the child were swept aside immediately and she would scold herself for being so selfish to consider herself in this manner, when it was only Violet who mattered.

Violet smiled at her and said, 'Can't you come too?'

Sister Assumpta felt her heart perform gymnastics. This was not the way she had chosen. She was aware of the plan to take Violet to a show and while she was mildly unsure of the plan, she knew that neither Bobbie nor Flynn would take her to anything inappropriate. In fact, their destination was not quite Shakespearean in subject. A little lighter and more musical. It was with a sigh of relief from the two Flynns when they heard Sister Assumpta answer the child.

'I have a lot of other girls to take care off, child,' replied Sister Assumpta kindly. 'But thank you for asking.' Her accent betrayed her Irish origins although she had been in America over forty years, the accent remained firmly rooted in Connemara.

She took Violet's hand and led her to the entrance hallway, which was dominated by a large religious painting and a small wooden crucifix. There were three photographs too: one of Pope Benedict XV, the recently deceased pontiff; the second was of President Warren G. Harding; the final one was of Padre Pio, a young Capuchin monk, whose hands and feet had developed wounds remarkably like those endured by Christ on the cross. His fame had spread globally and many in the church considered him a living saint.

Violet smiled when she saw Bobbie and was rewarded with a hug. Bobbie then glanced guiltily at Sister Assumpta.

'Forgive me, I should show more decorum,' she admitted with a rueful smile towards the nun.

'You should,' agreed Flynn grouchily.

'Oh, shush you,' said Violet and Sister Assumpta, in unison.

Flynn shushed.

3

Music Box Theatre, New York: 21st January 1922

The Music Box theatre, on West 45th Street, was one of Broadway's newest entertainment venues. It had opened in late 1921, a project of the songwriter Irving Berlin and the theatrical impresario, Sam H. Harris. Violet gasped as she and the two Flynns walked towards the limestone neo-Palladian entrance.

'Oh, my goodness, *"The Music Box Revue"*, I can't believe it,' exclaimed Violet excitedly.

'We thought you might prefer this to Julius Caesar,' explained Bobbie, who was holding the excited eleven-year-old's hand. 'And happy birthday.'

'I like Shakespeare,' said Violet who had turned eleven earlier in the week. 'I'd love to see the play.'

'I wouldn't,' grumbled Flynn.

'Ignore him,' advised Bobbie, rolling her eyes, but half-smiling.

'I shall,' said Violet, who knew how to play the game.

"The Music Box Revue" was meant to be a competitor to the very popular *"Ziegfeld Follies"*. All the songs were written by Irving Berlin and featured a mixture of song and dance numbers, as well as comedy. The show had been running to

packed houses since September, which, at least, gave Bobbie some confidence that it was worth seeing.

Two hours later they emerged from the theatre and even Flynn had to admit he had been royally entertained.

'What was your favourite bit?' asked Bobbie.

'I love that song,' and she began to sing a few bars of *"I'll Say It With Music"*, which was the hit song from the show. Flynn began to whistle it too, which brought a smile to Bobbie's face. Not only had she been worried about how Violet would react to the show, but she was also concerned that her father might be bored. It was clear her choice had been pitch perfect.

'Now for the second surprise,' said Bobbie.

Violet could hardly breathe with the sense of delight she was feeling. Even when she had been with the Belmonts, she had not enjoyed a treat like this one. She'd loved being part of a family but given that her own family had comprised an abusive drunk of a father and an alcoholic mother, the bar was not set very high. The feeling, if she could have put words to it at that moment, was not just a sense of excitement at what she had enjoyed that day. She also felt relaxed with the Flynns.

The father and daughter were a strange pair. He gave the impression of being crabby while Bobbie was young and full of sunshine. Yet they would snap at each other and happily make fun of the other's foibles. None of it seemed to bother them when they heard criticism. If anything, it would spur the other to respond in kind. Violet would often find herself laughing at the comments. This had not been the case with the Belmonts. Both, while very nice with her, had been quite formal and she always sensed a degree of tension in the air. This is why she enjoyed school so much.

The thought of school made her heart sink a little. She thought of her friend, Lydia Monk, for whom she had been mistaken and kidnapped. This had set off a chain of events that meant she had left the Belmonts and returned to the orphanage. The frenzy surrounding her return had calmed down, as the newspapers found another subject to sensationalise, but Violet was still feeling bereft. Or, at least, she had been. Now, she was beginning to feel something towards this young woman and her father.

And it scared her.

'Where are we going?' asked Violet.

'That would hardly make it much of a surprise,' pointed out Bobbie, as she hailed a cab. A yellow cab duly appeared immediately as it always did for Bobbie, which drew a sour look from her father who found that he was usually invisible as far as the cabbie breed were concerned. Or, perhaps, he was a little dismayed at the profligacy of his daughter for what was a shortish walk, albeit in the rain.

'Lindy's on 50th and Broadway, please,' said Bobbie, to the cab driver.

'I know it,' replied the cabbie, setting off.

A few minutes later, the cab deposited Bobbie and Violet outside the restaurant, while Flynn remained in the cab as he was returning to their Brownstone in Greenwich Village.

'Lindy's,' exclaimed Violet delightedly. This was rapidly becoming one of the best days of her life. She had heard of Lindy's and had always wanted to visit it. This had been turned down by her foster parents, the Belmonts, on the grounds that the restaurant was a haven for ne'er do wells which was probably not so far from the truth. Bobbie loved it there and one of the reasons was the person she was going to introduce to Violet.

They stepped in the through the metal and glass doors of the eatery. She immediately spied Damon Runyon, at his usual place, with the man he had promised to bring with him. Quite how he had managed this was not for Bobbie to inquire. Runyon's position as the most famous sports reporter in the city as well as his extraordinary relationship with the great and not good of the city meant that he knew everyone and everyone knew him. And liked him.

Bobbie saw a well-dressed dark-haired man beside her colleague. She took Violet by the hand and led her through the tables towards Runyon. Violet enjoyed watching the reaction of the men to the arrival of Bobbie. Her new friend was a looker by any estimation and Violet enjoyed seeing the effect she had on men of all ages. Although, for the little girl, none came close to the rather good-looking detective that she'd met on that awful day. What was his name? Then she remembered.

Nolan.

Before she realised it, they had arrived at the table. The two men stood up.

'Violet, can I introduce you to my friend and colleague, Damon Runyon.'

Runyon bowed formally with an impassive face. Violet felt a degree of uncertainty about who this man was. Then Runyon broke into a grin, saying, 'It is good to meet you, kid.' He held out his hand to Violet who frowned a little before shaking it.

'And my friend here is Mr Irving Berlin.'

Violet turned to the other man, who had a half-smile on his face. She stared at him for a moment in shock and then she turned to Bobbie, who was smiling. Finally, she was able to speak.

'I've just been to your show,' she announced.

'So, I gather,' replied the songwriter and creator of the *Music Box Revue*. 'I hope you liked it.'

'I loved it,' exclaimed Violet, excitedly.

'Could you write my next review,' said Berlin, taking a seat. Bobbie gently nudged Violet into the seat opposite the man who, in a short space of time, had written some of the biggest sheet music hits in living memory, including *Alexander's Ragtime Band*.

As much as Violet wanted to chat to Berlin about the show, the two men were fascinated by the kidnap. Violet, for once, was happy to oblige and was only interrupted in telling her story, which entertained the table royally, when a rather large ice cream arrived at the table.

While Violet tore into the latest treat, Bobbie talked about how much she had enjoyed the show. However, one issue had piqued her interest. There had been a minute's silence before the start of the show for a man she had never heard of.

'Who is George Rankin?' asked Bobbie.

Runyon and Berlin looked at one another and then pointedly at the child. Oddly, it was Violet who answered for Bobbie.

'Some guy that got clipped earlier,' replied Violet, which had the two men almost spluttering in shock.

'How did you know?' asked Bobbie, which was only one of a half dozen questions that she wanted to ask the child, another being how she had heard of the word 'clipped' used in this context. Then she remembered Violet's upbringing. She would have seen and listened to a lot worse than this.

'That is right, kid,' said Runyon. 'I guess there is no point in beating around the bush on this. Rankin was found dead in his apartment this morning.'

'And the minute's silence Mr Berlin?' asked Bobbie, her newspaper instincts were on full alert.

'I knew him,' said Berlin. 'He was a song plugger and a musician. His brother is in the orchestra for the show, but obviously he didn't appear today. Poor guy. He's pretty cut up.'

'I'm sure,' said Bobbie, who could not stop herself from finding out more.

'What happened to Mr Rankin? Was he murdered?'

'It sure sounds like it,' said Runyon. 'Someone shot him in the noggin.'

'How awful,' said Bobbie.

'You're telling me,' replied Runyon.

Demonstrating a degree of journalistic instinct herself, Violet polished off her sundae and asked, 'Was it a hit?'

Runyon felt they were way past protecting the child's innocent sensibilities and replied, 'I am sure our worthy men in uniform will determine such matters.'

Violet turned to Bobbie, her eyes wide with excitement, 'Do you think that cute detective will be on the case?'

The two men looked at Bobbie, a big grin on the writer's face. Bobbies face turned as red as her hair. Runyon fixed his eyes on Violet.

'What detective is this, kid?'

'Detective Nolan,' chimed Violet, before adding a comment that Bobbie might well have agreed with but would have preferred unaired at this point with someone like Runyon. Violet then added in a tone of mock awe, 'He's a dreamboat.'

'Dreamboat, eh?' responded Runyon, looking at Bobbie, eyes twinkling. 'How'd you know him?'

'He was on my kidnap case with Bobbie,' said the little stool pigeon. She was using her spoon now to mop up every last particle of ice cream on her plate.

'Do you think Bobbie likes him?' asked Runyon, mischief dripping from every syllable.

'Damon!' exclaimed Bobbie. 'That's quite enough.'

Violet was no amateur in the mischief stakes. She knew that she had stuck gold with this particular seam and she intended mining it for all it was worth.

'Well, if she doesn't then I do. I'll tell him to hold off on the dolls until I'm eighteen,' announced Violet.

'I thought you were already twenty,' said Bobbie, drily.

'I wish,' said Violet with mock sadness.

'Can we move on?' said Bobbie. 'Anyway, Violet, you should say "thanks" to Damon. He helped me a lot on your case.'

This seemed to cast a pall over Violet's mood, which Bobbie sensed and immediately felt guilty for raising the case. While Violet appeared to have come to terms with what had happened, there was one aspect of the case which, oddly, made her feel low and it was not related to her foster parents.

'Did you put the finger on Renat?' asked Violet.

Runyon had heard from Bobbie about this unusual aspect to the kidnapping and was on alert.

'Sorry, kid,' said Runyon and meant it. 'We have written very sympathetically about Renat the Russian.'

'I know,' said Violet, but this did not seem to give her any lift. She put the spoon down, as if losing her appetite for extracting every last drop of the sundae.

Damon smiled sympathetically to Bobbie, as he could see the regret on her face. Then he had an idea that would pick things up for the unusual little girl.

'Hey kid, what was that detective's name again?'

4

Midtown North precinct, New York: 22nd January 1922

The next day, Nolan strolled into the squad room of the station and sat down at his desk. He had to file his report on the previous day's activities, which had comprised speaking to over a dozen people connected to the former song plugger, George Rankin. They had now established his movements for the previous forty-eight hours. They had a list of people he had been in contact with, many of whom they had spoken to already, several they needed to locate.

There were a couple of other people there. As it was Sunday, Captain O'Riordan was off. He rarely worked Sundays, which was a surprise as he was not very religious. Invariably, the unmarried detectives were rostered for that day. The appearance of Sergeant Harrigan on that day was every bit as rare as the captain.

There were three men already in the squad room, Nolan's usual partner, Detective Yeats, Detective Fleischer and a recent arrival, Lieutenant Grimm, who was that and more. Grimm was as serious-minded as his name suggested and was destined, in the estimation of all who worked with him, for high places. This was less to do with his ability as a detective than a very smart approach to career management. While

O'Riordan harboured a similar ambition, he lacked the political nuance of Grimm. Neither man was popular, but most conceded O'Riordan knew his job. The jury was out on Grimm.

'Glad you could make it in this morning,' said Grimm to Nolan, as he saw the young detective arrive. Grimm was probably in his early thirties, but a combination of receding hairline, a very neat appearance, replete with rimless glasses, made him seem ten years older.

Nolan bit back his reply. He'd worked late into the night on the Rankin murder while Grimm was, no doubt, schmoozing with people who might further his career.

Nolan ignored the lieutenant's comment, merely nodding to him. He did the same with Yeats, but rolled his eyes while his head was turned away from Grimm.

'Anything new?' asked Nolan.

'You're even uglier first thing in the morning,' replied Yeats, who was built like a battleship and just as attractive.

'That would be a "no", then,' grinned Nolan, placing a sheet of paper in front of him, to write up a report on the previous day. He watched as the lieutenant approached his desk.

'What is happening with the Rankin murder, Nolan?' asked Grimm. His rimless glasses glinted malevolently in the light, like a dentist moments before an extraction.

Nolan quickly ran through what he and Yeats had covered, 'We've spoken to people in the building where he lives. They didn't see any visitors the previous evening. We've spoken with his brother. They weren't close. The brother is seven years older, has a family, plays in an orchestra at the Music Box Theatre on 45th. He saw Rankin occasionally but they never worked together despite both being musicians. No sweethearts, but I gather he saw girls from time to time. Still trying to get names. Yeats and I will go to the Ostrich Club today or tomorrow on 61st. He played in a band there. We'll visit his music publishers too. He was a song plugger for a couple of publishers. We'll see if we can dig up anything there, to add to the picture of his last twenty-four hours or anyone that might be able to suggest a motive.'

Grimm nodded at this. It all made sense, but he couldn't resist throwing in some ideas of his own.

'This is all about the motive, Nolan,' said Grimm. 'Find the motive and you'll have the killer.'

This was about as insightful as pointing out that the murder victim was dead. Nolan resisted looking in the direction of Yeats who, from the corner of Nolan's eye, he could see stroking his chin and nodding at every pearl of wisdom dispensed by the lieutenant.

The rest of the day was the sort of day that does not get written up in mystery books. It lacked a certain drama as Nolan and Yeats methodically built a picture of Rankin's last twenty-four hours, speaking to the people they had missed at his tenement and others that knew him, when they had an address.

The final person they spoke to was one of the band members they were able to track down, a singer by the name of Desi Monterey. Nolan assumed this wasn't his real name. The singer was from Puerto Rico originally but had settled in New York just five years previously. His black hair was lush, well coiffured and he had a pencil slim moustache, which he stroked proudly ever so often. There was a veritable cloud of fragrance surrounding him, mixed in with the vapours of his cigarettes which rarely left his lower lip. How do some people make them stick like that, wondered Nolan?

'Georgie is dead?' exclaimed Desi, dramatically, after Nolan broke the news to him in his apartment in Harlem. The news was, of course, tragic, but Desi gave it its due fuss. He clasped his hands together, his eyes widened, his nostrils probably dilated, but Nolan forgot to look. After the tears had subsided, and it was a few minutes, Nolan decided to start pushing things. It was late and he just wanted to go home and sleep.

'Do you know if George had any enemies?' asked Nolan.

'Not a soul,' said Desi, his hands trying to stem the tears in his eyes, his cigarette still locked to his bottom lip.

'You sure?' pressed Nolan. 'Someone must have had a problem with him.'

'Look he played with a few bands and they all liked him. He's a good guy. Was a good guy. He knew his music. Versatile too. He could play piano, sing, you name it. If you needed someone to fill in for you, you called George.'

'Do you know any of the bands he played with?' asked Yeats, who had been looking with increasing disenchantment at the melodramatic singer.

'He played with us two nights a week at Lavender's on 39th. I know he had a gig with Sammy Brown's Boys at the Ostrich Club. He played with a lot of folks though at one time or another, you know.'

Desi added a few more names to the list, which gave Nolan and Yeats more to follow up. This was the reality of police work. Not the dramatic intuitive jumps of gifted amateur detectives, but the slow grind of checking each lead, until it proved to be a dead end.

'What do you think?' asked Nolan, as they walked down the steps of the tenement. A few kids stopped playing and stared at them. One of them sent a few verbal missiles in their direction. The two men smiled back.

'Guy sickens me,' said Yeats.

'Desi Monterey?'

'Yes.'

'Why?'

Yeats looked askance at Nolan and said, 'He's one of them.'

That much had been clear to Nolan too, but he could have cared less and said as much.

'You're too good,' grinned Yeats, who liked his friend too much to require validation. 'Where to now?'

'Home. I'm dead beat,' said Nolan. He looked up at the ink-black sky and then around him at where they were. What a job, he thought, yet it was all he had ever wanted to do. He could have gone to college but chose this. Whatever you choose, it's probably wrong. And right. His father had owned and run his own shop for decades in New York. Worked every day. Hardly took a day off. He'd always told his son, before he passed away, not to worry about the choices you make, focus on the outcomes instead. Make your choice, stand by it, make it work.

Nolan had done just that. His mother never understood why such a smart boy would want to join the police. She was from Sicily. They made their own rules there. But Nolan had worked in the shop with his dad. He'd seen people trying to threaten his father, rip him off. Life was hard enough without the added pressure of extortion. His father should have been able to do his work free from fear.

So, Nolan had joined the police.

The two men travelled back to the station house. Yeats looked at Nolan and grinned ruefully.

'My turn?'

'That's my estimation. I wrote up yesterday.'

'I got Cindy tonight,' complained Yeats.

'I thought it was Shirley,' replied Nolan with a frown.

'That was last month. I mean it Sean, she's...' The feature that Yeats wished to convey about the young lady was rendered using his hands rather than articulated, which was probably just as well.

'Sounds charming,' said Nolan drily. 'Does she like French poetry?'

Yeats erupted in laughter, 'French letters mostly. C'mon buddy,' he pleaded. 'I said I'd meet her at seven. I'd do the same for you.'

Nolan shook his head and groaned at his friend, 'Get the hell out of here.'

'You're a pal,' laughed Yeats, clapping Nolan on the back nearly causing him to fly through the windscreen. Neither the friendly pat nor the comment, was much comfort to Nolan, who faced another hour of work thanks to their new lieutenant, who insisted on seeing a write up of the previous day's activities on his desk the next morning. He would then forward them on to Captain O'Riordan and Inspector Flynn. This was how you made promotion. Being organised.

'You owe me,' said Nolan to the empty seat beside him. He was smiling as he said it. Then he added dolefully, 'Cindy? Where does that dumb mutt find them?'

5

New York Tribune building, New York: 23rd January 1922

Around nine thirty the next morning, Bobbie Flynn stared down at her typewriter, where she had been dashing off an updated obituary, for someone yet to pass away. In this case it was the Pope, Benedict XV, who reports from Italy suggested, was about to find out if his life's work had been in vain or not. This was a part of her job that she was conflicted about.

She was genuinely interested in the lives of the great and the good; she enjoyed the research, almost as an extension of her real interest; detective work. However, there was a certain morbidity in writing about living people in the past tense which she found difficult. As a Roman Catholic, writing about the demise of the Pope who was still alive, made her feelings all the more acute.

She read through the changes she had made and decided they passed muster. In the background, she could hear the much slower typing of her boss, the head of "Obits", Buckner Fanley, engaged in similar work. When notable deaths were few and far between, they used the time to update their extensive library of future "customers".

Bobbie listened to the hypnotic, slow, percussive beat of Fanley's fingers on the keys, followed by the clack-clack-clack and then the ding, as he reached the end of a sentence. The deliberateness of his typing seemed an act of rebellion against her own rapid strokes and fast work. In her humble view, she got through three times the work that he did.

Finally, he finished and, almost apologetically, pulled the finished work from the wheel of the typewriter. He held it up in the air and viewed it as if he were in possession of a Raphael silverpoint. Then he set it down and glanced towards his subordinate.

Buckner Fanley was a man who had, probably, never been younger than sixty. His head was a bald dome, from which a few strands of grey hair clung on heroically, albeit for reasons surpassing understanding, over each ear. He wore round rimless glasses and might have seemed like a kindly uncle or mad professor, were it not for the deep crevice running from the side of his nostril to his mouth, which gave the appearance of a sneer. Fanley made every effort to live up to what Mother Nature had bestowed upon his appearance. He wasn't easily pleased and keen that you knew it.

'What have you there?' asked Fanley, looking with distaste at the sheaf of papers, beside Bobbie.

'Pope Benedict XV, Irving Berlin and O. Bonaty, Mr Fanley.'

'I don't remember asking you to update them,' said Fanley, with a frown.

'You didn't, but as I had the time and you were busy, I thought I'd keep active,' said Bobbie, with the innocent air of a woman who has made a damning point about female productivity, compared to the more leisurely chap. Fanley either did not understand the jibe or could care less. Being a male, both were equally possible. It made him even more frustrating for Bobbie, who had no less intention than drawing blood.

'Who is O. Bonaty, might I ask? I've heard of Berlin.'

This was her chance and she was going to take it. She desperately wanted to escape the dark, appropriately tomb-like atmosphere of the Obits Office and get out into the sunlight. And to be on a case.

'No one knows, Mr Fanley. He's the writer of the songs in the show, "*Heaven's Below.*" Are you familiar with it?'

'Is it likely to be on the repertoire of the Met?' sneered Fanley.

Bobbie laughed, genuinely, 'I hardly think so, but it's been playing to packed houses at the Jackson Theatre. No one knows who Bonaty is or where he came from. He's a genuine enigma. Refuses to meet the press. Works entirely through his lawyer. A complete recluse. The press is fascinated.'

'I believe I am part of the press, as you call it,' pointed out Fanley. 'And I couldn't be less fascinated about someone who pens lamentable popular ditties that sound like a cat in mid-yowl. Most of these writers excel only in their ability to outdo one another in their banality.'

Well, that was probably why Fanley had never been asked to be an arts critic, thought Bobbie. Now was the moment to press her suit.

'There was renewed interest, I noticed in some of the papers today, following the death of George Rankin. There had been rumours he was actually Mr Bonaty.'

'George who?' asked Fanley, taking off his glasses. This was a sign that he was interested.

Bobbie had her target in sight now.

'Yes, he was a musician and song plugger for the music publishing houses on Tin Pan Alley. He worked with the same publishing house that Bonaty does.'

'You seem to know a lot about it,' said Fanley, a trace of suspicion in his voice. Bobbie picked up on this. She had to tread carefully.

'I was at a show on Saturday and I heard about it then,' replied Bobbie, sticking closely to the truth.

'Should we write something on this Rankin? Has anyone else?'

Bingo!

'The papers have covered his death, but there have been no obituaries so far.'

Fanley thought for a moment. Then he puffed his cheeks and exhaled. He put his glasses back on. This could indicate only one thing: a decision had been made. Bobbie held her breath. She arranged her desk as if she had not a care in the world beyond the next death. She sensed Fanley was studying her. One good thing, that she would concede about the man, was that when he studied her it was done in a very different way from most men.

His assessment of her was not based on how she looked, or perhaps it was, but his reaction was very different to most men. Out of the corner of her eye she saw a slight shake of his head. It was the kind of movement one makes when you know you'll regret a decision. Her hopes shot up.

'Perhaps you should go out and see what you can find. Have it written up and on my desk by four.'

Bobbie skipped down the steps of the Tribune building with a feeling of freedom that matched that of a student on the last day of term. On top of this, her plan had survived contact with the enemy thus giving lie to Von Moltke's dictum on such a likelihood. She would make use of the time to follow up on the case. And make no mistake, this was a case.

The previous two days of the weekend had been idyllic and been spent with Violet. They were growing closer with each meeting, but Bobbie was keen not to push the young girl too quickly. She'd been through so much in her short life. Yet, even going into the office in the morning, she felt a stab of regret that she would not see Violet again until next Saturday. She would remain at the orphanage and be tutored by Sister Assumpta.

Bobbie could see the regret in Violet's eyes too when they parted the previous afternoon. Her father had been his usual grumpy self, but she could tell he was rather taken with the young girl. Violet had a wicked sense of humour that could puncture a balloon from fifty paces. Bobbie had seen her father fighting to stifle his laughter at some of her comments, even when they were hurled, malevolently, in his direction. Eleven years old and she understood Bobby's father, and he understood her.

Despite being with Violet, she had been able to formulate a plan for the next day, assuming she was able to intrigue Fanley sufficiently about the reclusive songwriter, Bonaty. While Fanley was male enough to resent her presence, he was newspaperman enough to recognise a story. There was a possible story here that could be dressed in an obituary's clothes.

Sometimes Fanley could surprise her.

A cab appeared as Bobbie reached the sidewalk. They usually did. It was almost magical and nothing to do with the fact that she had unfashionably long auburn hair, green eyes that were arranged rather nicely around a perfectly shaped nose and lips that were kissable by any estimation.

'Leo Feist's,' said Bobbie, before adding an address which was in the heart of the area that had become known simply as Tin Pan Alley. The term was coined by a journalist who thought the sound of cheap, upright pianos playing in the many music publishers' offices, in the area around 28th Street and 5th Avenue, sounded like tin cans banging in an alley.

They reached the offices after a slow grind through the traffic of Manhattan. Bobbie paid the cabbie and leapt out into the cold air. She shivered a little. Although the snow had cleared and the days were becoming a little longer it was still colder than a banker's heart. She inhaled the chilly air and felt it track all the way down to her toes.

As the cab sped off, Bobbie looked up at 28th Street with all the music publishers. There were around a dozen, maybe more. She set off in search of the one she wanted. Despite the legend surrounding its name, Bobbie could only hear New York traffic, rather than tin cans clanking. She felt a stab of disappointment at this. Soon she was at Leo Feist's. She took a deep breath and entered the offices.

6

Bobbie walked up to the reception where a woman, in her early thirties, stood waiting with an expression of bemusement. Perhaps she was more used to seeing young men clutching a sheet of dreams than a well-dressed attractive young woman. It made Bobbie wonder if there were many female songwriters in the industry. She'd never heard of any.

This made her feel unaccountably sad. The famous writers were all men. People like Irving Berlin who, thanks to Damon Runyon, she'd met. There was also Jerome Kern and PG Wodehouse and Charles K Harris. The latter had created the most famous song of the early twentieth century, "*After the Ball*". The new writers coming through were also men, people like the Gershwin brothers and the mysterious O. Bonaty.

'May I help you?' asked the woman at the desk.

'Yes, please,' replied Bobbie. 'I am Roberta Flynn from the *New York American*. I would like to speak with someone who can help me with an obituary I'm preparing, about George Rankin. I gather he was a regular visitor to your business.'

The woman seemed taken aback by Bobbie's request. It wasn't clear if this was because Bobbie was a woman and a journalist or because she had not heard of George Rankin's death. Bobbie hoped it wasn't because she hadn't heard Rankin's name before.'

'I hadn't realised. How terrible,' said the woman. 'Mr Rankin is dead?'

'Yes,' said Bobbie. 'This weekend.' She stopped at this point and decided not to mention that he'd been murdered. That might throw a different complexion on her arrival.

'How very sad,' said the woman and appeared to mean it. 'If you'll excuse me, I'll call up to the office and find out if someone can see you. Please take a seat.' She pointed to a wooden chair sitting by a coffee table. Overlooking the area was a large canvas in the modern style. It was a lot of coloured-in squares and rectangles and which might as well have been the work of a child than a great artist. The artist hadn't appeared to sign the front so Bobbie had no idea who was responsible.

She sat down on the chair which was beautiful and very much in the art deco style. It was horribly uncomfortable. To take her mind off the discomfort, Bobbie concentrated on listening to the sound of a piano playing upstairs. It was a little too indistinct to know if the song was any good or not.

A few minutes later the lady came from behind her desk and approached her.

'Mr Feist will see you now. If you would please go up the stairs you will be met there.'

Bobbie thanked the lady and walked up the stairs to the first floor. She was met there by another lady, who was a little older than her, perhaps thirty, quite attractive in a rather severe, professional way. Bobbie smiled and held out her hand.

'My name is Roberta Flynn. I'm from the *New York American*.'

'Good day Miss Flynn, my name is Miss Summer. We've only just been told the awful news about Mr Rankin. Is it really true?'

'I'm afraid so, Miss Summer,' said Bobbie. She could see that the woman was surprised and upset. Behind her glasses, the eyes glistened with tears. Bobbie wondered how well the woman knew Rankin. The young woman interested Bobbie because she tried to downplay her good looks by tying back her hair, wearing next to no makeup and by adopting a cold, professional exterior. Bobbie could identify with the desire to be taken seriously but being the proud possessor of auburn-red hair immediately attracted attention however unasked for.

'Come this way, Mr Feist can see you for a few moments and then I will introduce you to Mr Jones, who dealt with Mr Rankin.'

Bobbie followed the young woman into a large office which overlooked the street. The walls were covered with either photographs of the publisher with musicians and Broadway stars or sheet music artwork.

With the rise of parlour music in the 1860's came a realisation on the part of music publishers of the commercial value of printing advertising on the blank pages of music and adding a commissioned cover to the music to hook people attracted to the image. Invariably it was a romantic image of a couple or perhaps a star who was promoting a particular song or show. There was an upright piano by the door. It made Bobbie wonder if it had been placed there deliberately, to distract people as they entered, to put them off their game.

There were two men in the office. One was in his early fifties, slender with a dark suit and silver bow tie. His hair was turning to grey and he had a salt and pepper moustache. Bobbie presumed this was Mr Feist. He stepped forward and shook Bobbie's hand.

'Miss Flynn, my name is Leo Feist. This is one of my partners, Nick Jones.' Nick Jones was a little taller than Feist, around thirty, with fair hair and an open, friendly face. Unlike Feist, who was dressed conservatively in a dark suit, Jones wore a tweed jacket and a white polka dot blue bow tie.

'Hello Miss Flynn,' said Jones. He sounded like he was from Kansas.

Feist continued, 'Just after we heard of your arrival the New York Police Department were in contact with us. Is it really murder?'

'Yes, I'm afraid so, Mr Feist,' said Bobbie gravely. Now was the time to spring the deception. 'Of course, I don't want to take up your time or, indeed get in the way of the police. My dad is an inspector and I know how much they love the press getting involved.' This brought smiles to the others. 'I'd just like to hear a little bit about Mr Rankin so that we can give him an accurate obituary.'

As she was saying this, Bobbie hoped desperately that she was not turning a brighter red than her hair. How could anyone believe that a member of the press was seeking only to write an honest and truthful obituary when the deceased was a murder victim and rumoured to be the mysterious O. Bonaty?

'I'll be happy to help you, Miss Flynn,' said Jones, eagerly.

Apparently, someone could. The eager tone from Jones earned him a wry look from Miss Summer, but she remained silent.

Bobbie said her goodbyes to the eponymous head of the music publishers. Jones and Miss Summer led her through to another, smaller office. Like in the owner's office, Jones was keen on showing off the company's biggest sheet music successes, and they were a colourful array. One that attracted Bobbie's attention, featured the great Fanny Brice.

'Yes,' said Jones observing Bobbie's eyes, 'we work with some big stars. Please take a seat and tell me how we can help you.'

One other photograph attracted Bobbie's attention. It showed Jones wearing a uniform. His rank was sergeant. Another photograph beside this one showed a group of men sitting by an enormous gun. Bobbie guessed that this was a weapon they had captured, because all the men had dirt on their faces. One even had a bloodied bandage on his arm.

'So how can we help you?' asked Jones, opening a cigarette box and offering one to Bobbie. This was met with a shake of the head.

Miss Summers sat to the side of Jones' desk. Despite the glasses, the expression on her face remained neutral, but there was a sense of wry amusement at how easily Bobbie had managed to gain entrance and clearly interest Jones. Bobbie decided she quite liked Miss Summers.

'I was wondering if you could help me with the obituary. I need basic details like date of birth of course. Then if you could tell me about his role as a song plugger, that would be useful. Was he involved with any hit songs? There is also the rumour I heard about him being O. Bonaty. A comment on that would be useful, just to set the record straight. And finally, anything you know about the bands he played with. Anything really that can help tell the story of his life.'

A glance from Jones and Miss Summers was on her feet and walking towards a large wooden filing cabinet with dozens of drawers. She immediately extracted a card and read from it, earning further tacit approval from Bobbie for her capability.

'George Alexander Rankin. Born 1895 in Spokane, Washington,' said Mrs Summers, before looking up at Bobbie, who smiled and nodded back to her.

Jones smiled at his secretary, with just a hint of pride. It was always good to be seen to have a neat, ordered and efficient office. Especially in front of the press.

'So, Miss Flynn, before I speak about George, may I ask you what you know about the music publishing industry.'

'Not a great deal, I'm afraid. I love music and I often buy sheet music, although my skills on the piano are sadly neglected at the moment.'

Jones smiled benignly at this and continued, 'Well, as you may gather, we are sheet music publishers. In fact, we are one of the biggest in the country, if not the world. We have offices in many cities around the country. Sheet music is big business and it's only going to get bigger. With every new theatre that opens on Broadway, with every new show that is created, with every new star that is born, we have a chance to share the music of New York, not just with the country, but the world. Our company motto is "You can't go wrong, with any Feist Song", and it's true. We sell thousands of songs each week.'

'I hadn't realised just how big a business this is,' said Bobbie, scribbling notes down.

'It is and we are,' replied Jones, trying, and failing, not to sound smug about their success. 'Now, with this success comes some challenges. Many songwriters will come to New York to seek their fortune. And why not? It's the centre of the music world right now. To avoid being inundated with unsolicited songs, we work through song pluggers who act as a filter, I suppose, to ensure that we hear only a fraction of the songs out there but,' said Jones, pausing for effect, 'that fraction is the absolute *crème de la crème*. George Rankin was a trusted song plugger and had worked with us for six years, aside from when he volunteered in the War.'

Bobbie looked up in surprise.

'He was in Europe?' asked Bobbie, pen poised over her notepad.

'He was, and he saw action too. This makes his death even more tragic as he was, in my view, a genuine American patriot.'

'How terrible. To survive the War yet perish so sadly in New York.'

'Indeed,' agreed Jones. His voice cracked a little, making Bobbie realise that despite his rather self-satisfied demeanour, he was genuinely sad for what had happened to a fellow soldier.

'When he came back from France, we immediately took him on again. I had only just come back myself and I was delighted he'd made it through.'

'Had you known him before he went to the War?' asked Bobbie.

'Oh yes. I think we went over a few months apart.'

'You never met him over there?'

'No,' smiled Jones. 'There were rather a lot of us over there at the time. Anyway, he re-joined us in 1919. We have four song pluggers, that we use regularly and he was certainly one of our most trusted. He had a good ear for music and I know from the writers and other musicians, there was an appreciation of his talent. He was professional, could learn a piece very quickly and I'm sure Miss Summers will confirm, he had a fine voice that could turn to romantic ballads and comic songs with equal virtuosity.'

Bobbie noted that Miss Summers nodded at this. Clearly, Rankin had been liked and respected.

'As to George being the mysterious O. Bonaty, who can say? George did not come to us with these songs; that was Sol Maxim. But he says he was given them by a lawyer acting on behalf of Mr Bonaty. So, it could have been George, but it doesn't really stack up. Why the big secret? He already had a contract with us to plug songs, why make a whole big deal, when we would certainly have taken the songs anyway.'

'I haven't been to the show, are they good?' asked Bobbie.

'Well, they've certainly proved a hit at the Jackson Theatre. I like them myself, so too did Miss Summer.'

Miss Summer nodded at this but said nothing.

'I'm not buying that George was the writer. He'd have said something. So, for my money, you can put that rumour to bed, Miss Flynn,' laughed Jones, before becoming wistful again, as he realised such levity was, perhaps, in poor taste. He moved on to the final question asked by Bobbie, around the bands he played with.

'George played with a few bands. I think he played at the Ostrich Club, isn't that right Miss Summers?'

'Yes sir,' said Miss Summers dutifully. 'I can give you the details of who he played with and where.'

'Thank you, you're so kind.'

Outside in the corridor, they heard men's voices.

'That could be the police,' said Jones, leaping to his feet. 'Do you mind Miss Flynn, but I think duty calls.'

'I understand. I'm very grateful for all the help you've given me. I won't detain you any longer,' replied Bobbie, rising to her feet. They all went to the door. Jones opened it and allowed the two ladies to pass. There were other men in the corridor with Leo Feist. She heard him exclaim, 'Here's Jones now.'

Bobbie shook hands with Jones, who held her hand a little longer than etiquette required, fixed his eyes on her and said, 'please do call if you have any other questions. I'd be happy to help.'

'I shall,' said Bobbie, quickly extracting her hand, then she turned and walked straight into a tall man.

'Miss Flynn, what a surprise,' said a familiar voice.

7

'Detective Nolan, what a surprise, indeed,' said Bobbie looking up at the tall, good-looking detective.

'Do you two know each other?' asked Jones, hoping the trace of disappointment in his voice was not too obvious. It was picked up by Miss Summers whose head jerked in her boss's direction and a slight frown creased her forehead. As if in revenge she turned to Detective Nolan and fixed her eyes on him and smiled. Disconcertingly for Bobbie, she realised that Miss Summers had a very nice smile.

'I won't detain any of you,' said Bobbie waving her notebook in the air. 'I have all I need for the obituary on poor Mr Rankin.'

Leo Feist and Jones both smiled sadly, while Detective Nolan remained impassive. Yeats, on the other hand, had a slightly sceptical grin on his face, as he nodded to Bobbie.

'No doubt be seeing you again, ma'am,' he said, touching the brim of his hat.

Nolan, certainly, had no doubts about this but was unsure how he felt about the matter. He avoided glancing at Yeats but could see the half-smile on his friend's face.

As Bobbie headed down the stairs, she heard Nolan say, 'Miss Flynn is the daughter of Inspector Flynn who is technically the boss of mine and several precincts. We met on the Monk case.'

'Oh my, you were involved with that?' exclaimed Jones, but Bobbie had reached the bottom of the stairs and anything else was out of earshot.

As tempting as it was to hang around and catch up with the two detectives after their visit, she had seen enough in Yeats' smile to suggest that this would only put Nolan in a tricky spot and open him up to a few ribald remarks. She decided to have a think about what to do.

One thing was certain, and she had stopped even trying to deny to herself, that she was rather delighted to know that Nolan was on this case.

The only thing to do now was to head back to the Tribune building and post her obituary. It would take up some of the afternoon but not so much she could not plan out her next steps in becoming involved with the case.

She arrived back just as a few of the journalists were heading out to lunch. One of the men she saw, descending the steps, was a rather dishevelled man, in his thirties, known as 'Two-Brained' Toby. He was in his late thirties, tall, with straw-coloured hair and glasses that never quite seemed to sit straight on his face. He was in charge of crosswords and puzzles. The only puzzle to everyone was how someone so smart could barely dress himself sensibly.

'Hi Toby' said Bobbie brightly.

Toby stopped and looked at Bobbie. It usually took him a few seconds to reconnect with the world as his head was often elsewhere.

'Oh Bobbie, yes. Hi. What are you up to?'

'Nothing much. Just writing about the death of a young musician. I was hoping he would turn out to be the mysterious O. Bonaty, but I suspect that's a bust.'

'O who?' asked Toby, utterly bemused.

'You know, the songwriter. He wrote the songs for "*Heaven's Below*". It's quite popular.'

'Never heard of it. O, what?' asked Toby, still trying to focus his eyes on Bobbie.

'O. Bonaty. No one knows who he is. Probably this is why the show is sold out.'

'Why would anyone go to a show just because they don't know who wrote it?'

This made Bobbie laugh and she admitted that this was probably a fanciful idea. Then she added brightly, 'The songs are supposed to be good.'

'I'll take your word for it. Maybe I should take it in sometime. Sounds intriguing,' said Toby before giving a little wave and moving on. One good thing about Toby, like Buckner Fanley, or indeed, Thornton Kent the editor, he seemed not to view Bobbie as most of the men viewed her. To him she was a colleague. He knew vaguely what she did but was not in the least interested. She not only suspected, but she also knew, there was a book running on which of the newsmen would be the first to claim the red-headed prize.

They would be disappointed.

One of the things that Buckner Fanley, no doubt, would like to have complained about was the quality of Bobbie's work. This was another area where Bobbie proved disappointing to him. Her work was invariably well written, concise and lacked any hyperbole which he detested, as a rule. And she was quick. She snatched the paper from the typewriter and handed it over to Fanley, without waiting to see if he approved, or not. Of late, he had ceased correcting her work as, perhaps even to him, it seemed small-minded.

Or perhaps she was getting better.

The latter point was unlikely to be acknowledged by the mirthless martinet. And Fanley was too much of a married man to believe there was any point in trying to make any woman believe his influence had been instrumental in her development.

'What are you doing now?' asked Fanley, to the back of Bobbie.

'While I was in the world of music, I thought I might update a couple of the obits we have. I met Leo Feist today.'

'Who?'

'World's largest music publisher,' replied Bobbie.

'And yet, still not very famous,' retorted Fanley.

'I think you might hear a different story on Broadway.'

Even to Bobbie, this answer sounded weak so she disappeared to pick up a few of the files on famous music publishers like Feist or Charles K Harris, who had written "*After the Ball*" and had become one of the first songwriters to set himself up as a publisher, also.

Bobbie spent the rest of the afternoon immersed in the music world, familiarising herself with many of the personalities within the business side of the business rather than just the very public, front of house stars.

And an idea was now forming her in her head that terrified and thrilled her in equal measure. Around five in the afternoon she bid Fanley a good evening and set off before he had time to say, 'and where the hell do you think you're going?'

Around five thirty in the evening, Detectives Nolan and Yeats returned to Midtown North precinct. As they went up the steps of the station house, a newspaper boy grabbed Nolan and handed him a newspaper.

Nolan frowned at the boy and said, 'Sorry, son, I don't have time for a paper.'

'Yes, you do Detective Nolan,' said the boy.

This brought another frown. He looked at the front of the newspaper. It was the *New York American*. It was open on the Obituaries page. There was a note beside the headline.

MEET ME IN JAVA HEAVEN

Nolan glanced up at Yeats who was at the top of the steps.

'I'll see you inside Tim.'

Nolan watched Yeats turn and go while he gave the boy a quarter and then trotted across the road to beat the traffic, earning a whistle from a traffic patrolman. This made Nolan smile.

He walked inside the restaurant and saw her sitting alone in front of two coffees. He wandered over and sat opposite.

'That for me?' asked Nolan, gesturing towards the coffee.

'It is. Black, I seem to remember,' said Bobbie. 'I haven't added sugar.'

'Thanks,' said Nolan. 'So, to what do I owe the pleasure?' He knew the answer of course, but he was curious to see how she would broach it.

The question was met with a sceptical look. Nolan smiled and tried to look innocent. This brought a frown from Bobbie who had no choice but to come out into the open.

'I see you are working on the Rankin murder,' observed Bobbie.

'I am.'

'You've heard the rumour that he was really the mysterious O. Bonaty,' said Bobbie.

'I have.'

'They were dubious of this up at Feist's,' said Bobbie.

'So, I gather.'

This was like pulling teeth. Time to go direct.

'Any theories?'

'That I want to share with the press?'

That hurt a little and Nolan could see that it had. He immediately felt guilty for being quite so unfriendly. Now, Bobbie had observed the slight softening of his features and recognised the regret in his eyes. She was woman enough to feel his pain and then do what any sensible female, worthy of the description, would do - she went for the jugular.

'I wouldn't do that and you know it,' she said quietly, looking down at her coffee.

Nolan felt like he'd just been punched in the stomach by Jack Dempsey. The breath, and half his insides, seemed to evacuate his body and he knew he had to make amends quickly.

'That was low,' agreed Nolan, a hint of apology in his voice. 'No theories so far, to answer your question. No one saw who visited him. No one can provide a motive as to why someone should do this. He was liked well enough by the people who lived on his floor. Leo Feist said he was professional and good at his job. I haven't had a chance to speak to his band mates aside from one, Desi Monterey. He liked Rankin and knew of no one who had any desire to hurt him. At the moment it's a mystery.'

'I have a theory,' said Bobbie.

Normally, outside of the pages of a mystery novel, such a statement from a beautiful young journalist would be unlikely to be taken seriously by a detective. However, chance and murder had resulted in Detective Nolan seeing Bobbie not only helping, but also being instrumental in the solving of a crime. On at least one of those occasions, he had doubted, but persisted anyway, for reasons that were not hard to fathom and had little to do with any confidence that she was right.

'Go on,' said Nolan. His voice was neutral and there was none of the scepticism Bobbie had been expecting. It felt like she was being taken seriously. This provoked a number of emotions within her, that had her struggling to breathe.

'You won't laugh?' said Bobbie, just to check in and give him his final warning.

'I promise,' said Nolan, a hint of impatience, which was a reminder to Bobbie that he was still, technically, working.

'Have you considered the O. Bonaty angle?'

'Which is?'

'If we assume that Mr Rankin was not this mysterious writer, then what if he knew who it was and was threatening to reveal it?'

'Blackmail?'

'Yes. That would be a motive,' said Bobbie brightly.

'It would,' agreed Nolan, but he could not hide the doubt in his voice. 'Is that something worth killing over? I mean, does anyone really care who this O. Bonaty is? Even if the name was revealed and it was, say, Irving Berlin writing under a pen name, who really cares?'

This was slightly deflating, even for her, because this was where her theory fell down.

'Do you have to be so logical, Detective Nolan? You'll be asking for evidence next.'

'Annoying, I agree,' replied Nolan, a smile appearing on his face. His teeth were really quite even, noticed Bobbie.

This was not the end of the conversation. There was still one other purpose behind Bobbie meeting the detective. She stood up to signal the end of the meeting and they walked to the door of the restaurant. Nolan held the door open for Bobbie to pass.

The night air chilled them both, as they walked in silence towards the station house. Outside, Nolan turned to Bobbie and smiled ruefully.

'I have to...' he motioned with his head towards the building.

'I know. Anyway, I'll see you later.'

'Later?'

'Yes, you're taking me dancing?'

'Dancing?'

'Yes, the Ostrich Club. How else are you going to get in that place and not look like a cop? Pick me up at eight. You don't have to thank me.'

8

Bobbie applied the last piece of make up to her face, in a way that was designed to suggest that she was barely wearing any make up at all. She was about to walk out into the living room of the brownstone house she shared with her father, when she realised that her dress may provoke more than a raised eyebrow. This was a problem.

She opened the bedroom door and checked the corridor. The coast was clear. Hitching her dress up slightly, she dashed towards the stairs. Still no sign of anyone. She needed to reach her overcoat by the front door below. There was nothing else for it. She sprinted down the stairs towards the coat.

It was then she heard her father arriving on the corridor. Her heart was racing now. There were already a few risks she was running. There was nothing else for it. She fumbled with the coat and managed to slip it on just as he appeared in view.

'Where are you off to?' asked Flynn, seeing his daughter dressed up and at the door.

'Off dancing. I'm seeing some people tonight at the Ostrich Club. I won't be late.'

The Ostrich Club rang a bell with Flynn, but he couldn't remember why.

'Do you need me to take you?' asked her father.

'No, someone is collecting me,' said Bobbie.

This was both good news and bad news as any father would testify. He wanted his daughter to enjoy her life. Have fun. Do the things that young people did. Yet, as ever, there were qualms. Who was she with? Could he trust them? Of course, if she was with a chap then the answer was a resounding "no".

But what could he do?

And even if could do something, would he?

He knew the answer to that because he could hear his late wife, whispering in his ear – it's not your choice Flynn. She always called him Flynn.

He watched Bobbie disappear out of the door. Then he did what any self-respecting father worthy of the name would do. He rushed to the front room, without switching on the lights. From this vantage point, he was able to see the unmistakable figure of Detective Nolan, standing by a car. He was dressed in a tuxedo and even to Flynn's rather jaundiced eye, he looked very handsome indeed. They did not kiss, which was a relief and, instead, Bobbie climbed into the waiting car.

Flynn felt angry at what he'd seen. He felt very angry indeed. Moments later he strode over to the telephone and ripped the earpiece from the holder.

The Ostrich Club was located just off 43rd Street between 5th Avenue and Broadway. It was one of a dozen clubs that had a well-to-do clientele who liked to mix it a little with the Broadway crowd, comprised of members of the acting world, con men, gamblers and politicians. Whatever concerns Nolan felt about this venture, there was no question what a difference it made to have someone like Bobbie on your arm as you entered a nightspot. It was as if the Red Sea parted and the doormen moved out of the way. They even gave you a salute, rather than a snarl and a warning not to cause trouble.

Bobbie and Nolan marched down the stairs into the club, which was a speakeasy in all but name. Bobbie left her coat at the desk, while Nolan's eyes roved around the foyer of the club, which had a deep red velvety wallpaper and some photographs of notables who had visited, almost all of whom Nolan would happily have seen put inside.

They walked through double doors into a very large room. At the far end was a small orchestra. In front of them was the dance floor which was already full. Surrounding the dance floor were tables and chairs, covered in white tablecloths. A waiter led them to a table, not quite at the front of the dance floor. Nolan noticed how all the men in the room seemed to follow the arrival of Bobbie, all the way to the table.

'What can I get you?' asked the waiter, who was clearly from the Bronx.

Bobbie and Nolan looked at each other. Despite having a father who was a senior ranking policeman, Bobbie was not beyond enjoying a tipple on occasion. She knew her father did too. Prohibition existed, of course and it was impossible to ignore its consequences, but this was not to say one couldn't remind oneself of what the many politicians in the room had denied to the country.

'Lemonade,' said Bobbie demurely, not wanting to put Nolan in a difficult position.

'Make that two,' said Nolan, a little relieved.

'Last of the big spenders, huh?' said the waiter sourly. He marched off into the crowd.

'Shall we?' asked Bobbie, motioning with her eyes to the dance floor. Nolan raised one sceptical eyebrow at this. This made Bobbie grin and she added, 'I won't bite you. Anyway, we must pass the time somehow until they stop playing and we can talk to them.'

Nolan nodded at this. It made sense yet he still felt his chest tightening. He wasn't a bad dancer, but what was he dealing with here? This question had more than one meaning and, certainly, more than one answer.

Nolan weaved expertly though the dancers, holding Bobbie's hand, until they were near the orchestra. It was comprised of a drummer, a pianist, two trumpeters, a black, female singer and a saxophonist. There was small guitar, also, sitting by one of the trumpeters.

'Is this ok?' asked Nolan.

Bobbie nodded and put her hand on Nolan's shoulder. As shoulders went, it met with her approval. His shoulders were level with her nose and pleasingly wide. Nolan's problems were just beginning though. His eyes widened as he put his hand on Bobbie's back and found himself touching her skin. He hadn't noticed, or was studiously trying not to, that she was wearing a rather low-cut backless dress. The front of the dress blackly shimmered and, at first sight, appeared to be quite modest. The back was anything but. This was both a revelation and cause for concern.

'Something wrong?' asked Bobbie, fully aware of Nolan's dilemma.

Nolan managed to mumble an apology, which caused Bobbie's grin to widen. In an effort to find some dress to put his hand on, Nolan moved his hand lower and lower still. Was she wearing anything at the back?

Finally, his hand came to rest on a part of her dress at the lower base of Bobbie's spine. This gave him no comfort, as it was precariously close to replicating what an old man was doing nearby. He'd thrown caution to the wind and had clamped both his hands on his young partner's behind. Bobbie noted the line of Nolan's gaze.

'Tempted?' she asked innocently.

'No,' replied Nolan firmly.

Bobbie shrugged but said nothing to this. Instead, they did what everyone else around them was doing. They danced.

For around ten blissful minutes, the case was forgotten about. Although Nolan could not quite rid himself of his worries regarding hands, feet and everything in between, he did manage to find himself enjoying the dancing and he was thankfully not making a fool of himself.

The last dance before the break was announced. Bobbie and Nolan stayed up, for most of it, before returning to their table to refresh themselves with the lemonades brought by the waiter. Soon after, the band departed for their break. Bobbie and Nolan waited five minutes, to give the band time to get their drinks and return to the dressing room. Then Bobbie said, 'Shall we go to work?'

They walked over behind the bandstand and towards a corridor. There was a man about Nolan's height but much burlier, standing to block anyone coming in. Nolan flashed his badge and said, 'I just want a few minutes. Nothing to worry about.'

The man looked unhappy at this and then he glanced at Bobbie. The look he gave her made Nolan want to teach him some manners. He stood aside and let the two of them pass.

'I'll speak to the singer,' said Bobbie.

They parted company at the dressing rooms. Nolan knocked on the door of his room and heard someone shout to come in. Bobbie did likewise at the dressing room occupied by the singer.

'Come in.'

Bobbie walked in and found herself in a small dressing room. There was a table with a mirror, ringed with lightbulbs and a lady of about forty, taller than most men and better built too. She peered at Bobbie, in undisguised shock, through black eyelashes so full they might once have been an ostrich's feathers. Louella LaForge often said she was all woman and there was, certainly, a lot of woman in front of Bobbie, right at that moment.

'You lost honey? The boys room is the one just before mine,' the voice was an unusual mixture of honey and steel.

'I came to see Miss LaForge,' said Bobbie.

'The boys will be disappointed.'

'They'll get over it I'm sure,' said Bobbie, which provoked a booming laugh from the singer.

'Not if they see you, sweets, not if they see you. Now, what do you want?' Miss LaForge sat down on a stool and lit a cigarette. She offered one to Bobbie but was met with a shake of the head.

'I came with a detective tonight,' said Bobbie, and then held her hands up as she saw alarm in the singer's eyes. 'We're looking into George Rankin's murder. I was hoping you could help me.'

'I'd like to, but how?' said Miss LaForge. She seemed to mean it, so Bobbie pressed onward.

'The police are struggling with the motive. Everyone we've spoken to is shocked, by what happened and no one can suggest any reason why anyone would want to kill him.'

'I'm afraid I won't be able to help you more than they did. George was a straight guy. I liked him. He didn't mess around, you know, the way some men do. There was no prejudice. He came to do his job. We worked well together. Yes, I liked him. I can't imagine why anyone would do something like that. It's just so sad.'

Bobbie listened and nodded sympathetically. It was clear that she was moved by Rankin's death.

'So, he didn't have any enemies or professional jealousies?'

'Not that I was aware of honey. People liked him. He did his job. He went home.'

'Do you know who his friends were? Or girlfriends?'

The singer's face clouded over with doubt. She said, 'Hey look honey, I don't want to put anyone in trouble.'

'You do want to find his killer, though,' said Bobbie softly.

This brought a nod and then the singer said, 'There was no one special as far as I could tell. He saw Lucia from time to time.'

'Lucia?'

'Lucia Montez. She sings at the Lavender Club. He played with her there from time to time.'

'I thought they had a singer, Desi Monterey.'

'Lucia and Desi sang together. Or apart. It's a pretty loose arrangement we all have.'

'I see,' said Bobbie. 'There would have been no jealousy about Mr Rankin seeing Lucia?'

'Not from Desi if you take my meaning, I don't know about the boys in the band, though.'

Just at that moment they heard loud voices in the corridor. One of them sounded like Nolan. Bobbie excused herself and opened the door to find Nolan standing a foot away from a small, middle-aged man who was shouting at the detective. Nolan had a half-smile on his face and, clearly, could care less about the little man's remonstrations. Then Nolan glanced over towards Bobbie.

'I guess we're not welcome here.'

The older man turned to Bobbie and did a double take. Detectives sure didn't look like Bobbie normally and that was a pity in any man's book.

'Who's she?' demanded the man, a little less aggressively. Beside him the big man, who had originally tried to block them, looked on with violence in his eyes.

'His date,' answered Bobbie, with a smile and sidled down the corridor towards the two men and took Nolan's arm. 'Shall we go now?' She smiled at the man she presumed was the club owner and said, 'It was a pleasure to meet you.'

Bobbie felt Nolan take her hand and he led her away from the corridor. Now that he was away from the threat of violence, his face became quite grim.

'This was a mistake,' he said, turning to Bobbie. 'I could have put you in trouble.'

'Don't worry,' replied Bobbie. 'I can take care of myself.' Bobbie was not entirely sure how true this was but her voice sounded convincing, even if her heart was not quite so sure.

They reached the foyer of the club.

'I need to get my coat,' said Bobbie. 'You go outside. I'll see you there.'

Nolan was a little reluctant to do this, but he did not want to appear to be acting as a nanny towards the young woman.

He climbed the steps and was soon in the chill night air. Before he had time to breathe in the fresh air, he felt an arm encircle his neck and he was thrown roughly against the wall of the club.

Standing before him were two patrolmen. Neither looked in a very friendly mood.

9

It took Nolan less than a second, or two, to recover, first from the shock of being so badly manhandled and then from seeing who had done it. His mind went into overdrive. He didn't need to think long about what had happened. The club obviously had an "arrangement" with some patrolmen to ensure that it was protected from raids or, at least, had advance warning when the police were likely to come. Nolan and Bobbie's unorthodox evening had clearly thrown everyone into a panic.

One of the patrolmen stepped forward, he was holding a wooden baton. Now at this point the patrolman was more intent on threat than actual harm. The plan had been to grab the young blood detective by the lapels and give him a dose of reality when it came to such escapades. The last thing he was expecting was for the young cop to launch himself forward and connect with a beauty of a left hook that left the patrol man sprawling, semi-conscious, on the ground.

The second patrolman's mistake was in turning to his partner. By the time he realised his mistake, he had been almost lifted up and thrown against the wall by Nolan. The young detective's face was inches from the older patrolman.

'I faced a lot worse than you in Europe. Now, I don't know who you think you work for, but I work for the New York

Police Department and I am performing my duty. If I see you or your buddy near me again, I won't be so friendly, understand?'

This was something of a turnaround in roles and the patrolman was mute with shock at the unfolding events. He felt himself being pulled back and then slammed against the wall once more.

'I said, do you understand?' snarled Nolan. The patrolman nodded, too stunned to say anything. Nolan released him and then, pointing to the other patrolman lying on the ground, he said, 'Scrape that off the sidewalk and get the hell away from here. If I think that you, or buddy boy here, are looking to get a little revenge I'll get some of my pals from Midtown North to remind you who you work for.'

The mention of Midtown North brought a frown and then a smirk, from the patrolman. Nolan did not know what to make of that, so he remained silent, keeping his eyes fixed on the two men as they staggered off into the night. A few onlookers, a little the worse for drink, clapped ironically.

Nolan turned to the entrance to find Bobbie standing looking at him thoughtfully.

'Looks like I can't leave you alone for a minute Detective Nolan,' said Bobbie, before turning and walking in the direction of the car that was parked further up the street.

Inside the car, Nolan was too wound up by the scuffle outside the club to speak. Bobbie, sensing that he was somewhat discomposed, left him to start the car and set off.

'What was all that about?' she asked.

Nolan suspected her question had wider meaning than just the encounter outside.

'It seems club owners don't like cops like me coming in unannounced and asking questions. I should never have brought you.'

'Nonsense,' said Bobbie cutting him off. This was not a subject she wanted pursued. 'What did you learn from the guys in the band?'

'No enemies. No motive from anyone they knew. They did say he'd been a little upset recently, though.'

'Why?' asked Bobbie, leaning towards Nolan. This was disconcerting for the detective. The fragrance she was wearing was already on his tuxedo and the memory of the pleasant curve of her spine was all too vivid.

'A friend of his had died. They gave me a name, Matt Nicholls. The police said natural causes, but Rankin thinks the guy was murdered. How about you?'

'Same. No enemies. No motive. I did get the name of a girl, though. Sometimes sings with his band at the Lavender Club.'

'Lucia Montez?'

'Oh,' said Bobbie, a little deflated.

'Desi Monterey mentioned her. Girlfriend?' asked Nolan.

'I don't think it was a firm arrangement by the sounds of it,' said Bobbie.

Nolan grinned and turned to Bobbie. He said, 'It doesn't sound like you approve.'

Bobbie coloured a little at this and replied, 'I don't know that I implied that.'

'Yes, you did,' laughed Nolan.

This brought a few moments silence from his passenger. Nolan left it like that to see how Bobbie would respond.

'I suppose I don't know what's in it for her. He has his fun and, well...'

Nolan's smile widened, 'You're quite old-fashioned, aren't you?'

'Not that much,' said Bobbie, stiffening, but she sounded defensive and unconvincing, even to her own ears. 'I suppose I'm still an Irish Catholic girl at heart,' she admitted finally, with a chuckle.

Nolan nodded at this but chose not to tease her any further on the topic. Bobbie, keen to move back to the case, dived into her next suggestion, like a six-year-old at a swimming pool.

'So, when are we going to see Miss Montez?' asked Bobbie, holding her breath.

'We?'

'We. Don't you think that I'm more likely to get something out of this young woman than two big cops.' The fact that Nolan could, probably, get any young woman to open up, was something that she didn't care to think about.

Nolan was cop enough to be appalled at the idea of Bobbie's continued involvement in the case, especially after the altercation at the club, and humble enough to recognise that she probably could get more from a young woman than he. Something in his silence alerted Bobbie that she might be losing the battle of wills.

'I understand your reluctance. But you must realise that women will one day work alongside the police as equal partners. We can bring things that men, frankly, do not seem interested in. We are empathetic. We are detailed. We are analytical. We are...'

'Difficult,' suggested Nolan. The smile was still on his face.

Bobbie erupted into laughter. When she had finished laughing, she acknowledged the truth of this.

'We can be, I suppose. Is that a bad thing to be, though?' she said, defiantly.

So far, so true, but the one great problem remained, as yet, unarticulated.

'And your father?' murmured Nolan, as much to himself as to Bobbie.

This did not slow Bobbie's momentum so much as bring it crashing against a brick wall. Yet, she had an answer to this too.

'I'm twenty-one. I can make my own decisions,' she turned to Nolan as she said this and fixed her eyes, rather disconcertingly, on his. She had nice eyes, thought Nolan. Green. Bobbie's thoughts were almost identical to his, regarding Nolan's own ocular attributes. She continued her thought, 'But I accept that it may put you in a difficult position, from time to time.'

'I'll say,' agreed Nolan, but it was not unkind or meant to be self-pitying.

'Ultimately, my father will judge you on results,' pointed out Bobbie.

Nolan shook his head and eyed Bobbie. He said, 'No, Miss Flynn. If anything happens to you then the results will not matter to him. Or if I were to beat the heck out of some guy to get a confession, I doubt your father would be impressed. No, Miss Flynn. Results are important, but your safety and staying within the law, are also important.'

Bobbie sensed defeat was imminent. A knockout blow waiting to be delivered. When in doubt, attack. That was her motto. Well, at that moment it was.

'I think that Miss Montez is a safe bet, don't you? My point still stands. She'll talk to me.'

'I can't stop you going to see her,' admitted Nolan.

This would hardly do, thought Bobbie. It was a much more enticing prospect going with the young detective. Time to be a little more direct in her appeal.

'I could,' agreed Bobbie. 'I think if we went together, we might get more.'

'Why?'

Bobbie was silent for a moment. Her breathing was becoming a little bit of a struggle. She had to say it and there was no point in beating around this particular elephant in the bush.

'You are, if I may say, probably someone who a young woman might consider attractive,' said Bobbie hurriedly. She ignored the arched eyebrow and pressed on. 'For that reason, you may be trusted more than, say, an old grump, like my father, dealing with a young woman.'

'You want me to flirt with her?' grinned Nolan.

This definitely would not do, but a part of Bobbie was curious to see how he would do this, as he had, so far, resolutely failed to do so with her, even when his hand had been perched delightfully close to her posterior when they had danced.

'I think, between the two of us, we could get her to talk about what was worrying Mr Rankin. A little bit of girl talks and, maybe, the charm of Detective Nolan might do the trick.'

'Charm?'

'Just because you are coldly professional with me, doesn't mean there may not be some aptitude to make yourself agreeable to a woman, if you put your mind to it,' said Bobbie, staring straight ahead at the road.

This stung Nolan a little. As ever, for the chap of the species, he was slap bang in the middle of an impossible position, when it came to dealing with the opposite sex. To this he said nothing and they travelled the rest of the journey, back to the Flynn household, in an uncomfortable silence.

Bobbie said a curt goodbye to Nolan and she skipped up the steps of the big brownstone house. She was through the door without a backward glance towards Nolan. The detective noted this, but felt duty bound to ensure she was inside safely before departing.

Inside the house, Bobbie felt a strange mixture of frustration and even elation. She had enjoyed dancing with Nolan. The memory of his touch made her feel almost giddy with happiness. Yet, to the extent that she had been delighted by the dancing, she was in despair about how she could further inveigle herself into the investigation. Nolan seemed to have shut the door on her.

This situation was about to become a whole lot worse.

After a few moments, she was aware that she was not alone in the corridor. She looked up and saw her father standing looking at her. Luckily, her coat was still on so he was not treated to the same expanse of skin that Nolan had certainly enjoyed viewing earlier in the evening.

Bobbie could read the anger in his eyes.

Attack.

'Is something wrong father? It's barely half ten. I'm hardly very late,' said Bobbie. Her tone was sharp enough to act as a warning to her father. If she had hoped this would give him pause for thought, she was to be very mistaken.

'Enjoy your evening with Detective Nolan?'

Ahh, thought Bobbie. Best be on my guard.

'Yes, I was out dancing with Detective Nolan, daddy. Is there a problem with this?' Her tone was just shy of outright rebellion now. There was a line in the sand when it came to her dates. Bobbie's view was that she had full discretion over choice, but with the proviso that her father could probably deploy a veto when the young man was clearly unsuitable.

Where did Nolan fit in this scenario?

'Yes, there is Bobbie and you well know it.'

'Do I?' exclaimed Bobbie. 'Mom dated you, against her father's wishes. You were no more senior than Detective Nolan is now.'

Flynn stepped forward, there was a fire raging in his eyes. Bobbie wondered if she'd overstepped the mark with a mention of her late mother, a socialite who had scandalised her family by marrying the policeman who had saved her life. The family had forgiven her and Flynn, in the end, but the first few years had been tough.

'That's not my point,' hissed Flynn, in a malevolent whisper. 'Do you think I'm stupid? Do you not think I know what you're doing? You're using Nolan to get access to the Rankin case. You have no right to use him like that. You have no right to risk both of your lives on these escapades. Where were you? Out at a club where Rankin used to perform? Do you know what sort of people run these clubs?'

Bobbie was feeling a little ashamed now. She had used Nolan somewhat, although her reasons for doing so were a lot more complicated than she was prepared to own up to, in front of her father. And he was right. Bobbie had seen, first-hand, what sort of people ran these clubs. While Nolan had handled the situation well, her presence might have undermined him. Guilty tears stung her eyes now. But Flynn wasn't finished.

'It's not about you, Bobbie. It's about Nolan too. If something happened to you that would be the end of his career. There would be no way back for him. He's good. He has a chance at a decent career ahead of him, but I promise you, Bobbie, if you get mixed up with him again on this case I will bust him back down to the street. He will be hearing from me tomorrow. You will be dead to him.'

Bobbie had heard enough now. She ran past her father and up the stairs, unable to hide her despair any longer. Flynn watched her run past him and felt like he'd been smacked in the stomach repeatedly by baton.

What was he doing wrong?

10

Flynn household, New York: 24th January 1922

Bobbie was spared an awkward encounter with her father at breakfast, by the fact that he left early. This was good insofar as it gave both time to cool off from the previous night's encounter. However, Bobbie had no doubt that he would be heading to Midtown North precinct, at some point in the morning, to confront Detective Nolan about involving her in a live murder case.

The more Bobbie thought about it, the more she realised that this was unavoidable. She felt wretched. It was one thing to have an argument with her father over boyfriends; it was quite another to sacrifice a young man's career on the altar of her ambition. She knew that, if anything happened to Nolan, it would spell the end for her desire to become a crime reporter. The idea would be sullied beyond repair.

Her trip, into the Tribune building, was made with an increasing sense of dread. Until she knew that Nolan's career would not to be capsized by their antics of the previous evening, then she knew an anxious day lay ahead of her. The thought of spending her time in a gloomy office with Buckner Fanley was not the balm needed at that moment.

One of the unacknowledged benefits of working with Fanley was the fact he appeared not to care what she did, if she delivered the right copy, on time, without undue hyperbole or any grammatical errors. In this, Bobbie was as much of a pedant as her boss was.

She arrived at the office just after eight thirty in the morning. This was much earlier than the official start time. This was another area in which Fanley could find little fault with his subordinate. Had he been forced to the ground and threatened with a pickaxe, he might have, reluctantly, admitted to trusting Bobbie. This would never be offered spontaneously of course.

'Is there anything you want me to work on today, Mr Fanley?' asked Bobbie, as she sat down.

'Library,' said Fanley. This, rather succinct, reply contained within it quite a few things that would need to be attended to. Aside from writing obituaries or updating existing ones, from time to time there was the need to keep up to date with their understanding of things that could be used across multiple articles. This was a rather dry exercise in acquiring data on the economy, on business sectors, on companies, invariably large like financial institutions, retailers and railroads.

Even though it was a rather dull activity at the best of times, Bobbie felt her heart suddenly lighten at the prospect of being away from the office, doing something useful.

Bobbie caught a cab and, immediately, made her way to the Midtown North precinct. Her intention was not to confront Nolan nor to apologise, yet. She had another plan in mind. The journey took ten minutes and soon she was sitting having a coffee by the window opposite the precinct. The plan, such as it was, involved following Nolan to the young woman that she had helped identify from her conversation with the singer, Lucia Montez. She was gambling Nolan would make her one of the first people he saw.

A few minutes later a car pulled up and out stepped her father. Bobbie quickly put her hand in front of her face, lest he see her. The man had the eyes of an eagle and missed nothing. Growing up had been a nightmare as he was the one person she could never fool. Nothing much had changed now she was twenty-one.

The heaviness she had felt earlier in the morning returned to her. There could be only one reason for his visit that morning. Feelings of guilt swept over her. She wondered what he would say to Detective Nolan.

Inspector Flynn flew up the stairs of the precinct nearly taking out two patrolmen in the process. He flew into the squad room and looked around him. Sergeant Harrigan saluted him with a cigar he'd stolen from the Commissioner, while he was on the phone.

Lieutenant Grimm was on his feet immediately and marched over to greet Flynn. The sight of the inspector was not so unusual at the station. He was a frequent visitor and was well known for taking an interest in the cases that the men had on. Flynn turned towards Grimm and shook his hand.

'How's tricks?' asked Flynn. The inspector was unsure about Grimm. The man had every appearance of being a martinet. Yet, he could not criticise him for dressing neatly, with an almost military like precision in his conduct. There were enough bad apples around the NYPD, he did not have that sense from Grimm. The man was too ambitious to sully himself by getting involved, as many cops had, with the underworld.

'All the better for seeing you, sir,' replied Grimm. Perhaps this was why Flynn was so unsure. Grimm's manner was professional, yet it also did not so much border on sycophancy, with superiors, as jump two-footed into fully-fledged obsequiousness. A few of the men in the room looked up, upon hearing this remark from Grimm and shook their heads. One of them was Nolan. Unfortunately, he was doing this just as he caught Flynn's eye. And it required no great effort of deduction, on the young man's part, to see the anger.

'Tell me about what you have on,' said Flynn, leading Grimm into the lieutenant's office. Flynn stayed for a round five minutes before he had had enough.

'Have you seen my daily reports, sir?' asked Grimm as Flynn edged towards the door. This had become both a feature and a bane of life, for the men at Midtown North. Grimm insisted that they finish off their reports for the day and have them on his desk first thing next morning. In triplicate. He sent off one copy to 240 Centre Street, where the Commissioner and Flynn worked.

'I have,' growled Flynn. 'Look, I've been wanting to talk to you about that. I don't mind that you want to get the men to be more structured than they have been in the past. Lord knows, it can be the Wild West. But I'd rather have more men out solving crimes, than writing reports. Find a better balance son. No one has time for all this paperwork, certainly not me.'

At that point he escaped from the office, leaving Grimm to chew on the parting shot. Flynn headed towards the exit of the squad room, pausing only a moment to fix his eyes on Nolan and gesture him to follow.

Nolan was on his feet in a moment. He ignored the grins from Harrigan and Yeats who both suspected, but could not be certain, that the subject might involve the rather attractive daughter of the inspector. Yeats had also noticed Bobbie, the day before and given his partner merry hell over her interest.

Outside in the corridor, Flynn took a moment to check that no one was around to hear what he was about to say. Nolan stood in front of the inspector. Looking up at the tall detective, Flynn had to acknowledge he was a fine-looking young man. It was easy to see how a young girl's head might be turned. Young woman, he reminded himself bitterly.

'Do I need to tell you that your escapade last night cannot be repeated?' snarled Flynn, at Nolan.

Nolan sighed and replied, 'No sir. I'm sorry. It won't happen again.'

Flynn jabbed his finger into the breast of Nolan. 'You better be playing straight with me son. Otherwise, I'll bust you down to traffic cop. In Schenectady.'

'Yes sir,' said Nolan, hoping that this signalled the end of the dressing down. It did.

'Tell me about this Rankin case. What's the story?'

Nolan, quickly and concisely, provided the key details of the case. Flynn listened in silence, as Nolan related what they had done so far. He nodded once or twice and then asked the question uppermost in his mind.

'And what is my daughter's theory on this?'

The tone of the question was somewhere between the exasperation of the father of an errant daughter and genuine curiosity. Sadly, for Flynn, his daughter appeared to have inherited many of his own qualities of intuition and the ability to see beyond the confines of a crime scene and into the cracks where motive and opportunity lay. For a father, whose pre-eminent desire was for his daughter to be as far away from the crime desk as possible, this was somewhat infuriating.

Nolan paused for a moment, to collect his thoughts, then he began to speak.

'Miss Flynn believes there is a connection between the death of George Rankin and the songwriter O. Bonaty.'

'Who?' asked Flynn, utterly bemused.

Nolan explained who Bonaty was and the songwriter's connection between Rankin and the music publisher, Leo Feist.

'So, no one knows who this is?' asked Flynn, not sure why he was pursuing the subject.

'No. Feist doesn't know. I gather that even Bonaty's representative does not know.'

'Who represents this Bonaty?'

'A law firm. Ben Strauss,' replied Nolan.

'Are you going to go and see this guy?'

And here lay the crux of the conversation. To do so would be for Nolan to admit that, once more, Bobbie's instincts were leading him. How this would go down, with her father, lord only knew. Nolan was silent for a moment then Flynn spoke once more.

'Perhaps you should.'

'Yes sir.'

'When are you seeing Miss Montez?' asked Flynn.

'This morning.'

Flynn nodded to this and then he fixed his eyes on the young man, once more. Nolan girded himself for another reprimand.

'There's something else, Nolan, I need to talk to you about. Walk with me.'

11

Around half an hour after he had arrived, Bobbie saw her father leave the precinct. A few minutes later Detectives Nolan and Yeats appeared. They walked towards a parked police car. Bobbie was on her feet in seconds and rushed outside. She hailed a cab and within a few moments she was on the tail of the detectives.

They drove through Manhattan, up towards Harlem, arriving at a neighbourhood that was like a ravine of tenements. The two policemen stepped out of the car. For one moment Bobbie thought she was caught by Nolan, but his eyes were just scanning the street. They stepped into the building, leaving Bobbie unsure if she should leave the safety of the cab or risk going outside.

She decided on the latter, paid the driver and walked towards the building. There was nothing at the front to indicate if this was where Lucia Montez lived. As the lobby of the building was empty, she ran up the steps and went inside, to see if she could find a post box that would show, one way or another, if this is who the two detectives had come to see or if it was another person connected with the case.

The post boxes had name tags on them and, to Bobbie's relief, one of them read Lucia Montez. She noted the apartment number and then quickly exited the building in case the detectives returned.

Further down the street was a garden that allowed public access. She went inside and sat down. Now all she had to do was wait. Easier said than done. Tailing people may sound like an exciting nerve-wracking activity. It is. Mid-winter New York is also desperately cold. More sensible denizens of the city were wrapped up warm and snug, with a coffee to heat hand and heart. At Christmas, the chill air carried with it the crisp fragrance of holiday cheer. Late January was altogether less fortifying to the spirit. Bobbie felt miserable, cold and genuinely brooded over the wisdom of her ambitions regarding a position on the crime desk.

The park was empty, except for a few curious birds which wandered over in Bobbie's direction, no doubt seeking food. They were to be disappointed. Finally, after half an hour of slowly freezing in the park, the two detectives emerged. This was good news. It meant that Lucia Montez had been in and responded to questions.

Bobbie quickly turned away lest she should be spotted. She would wait two minutes and then head over to the building, to try her luck in interviewing the singer. As she waited, she sensed, rather than heard, footsteps and someone coming towards the seat. She kept her eyes fixed resolutely ahead.

Someone sat down beside her.

A man.

'Hello, Miss Flynn,' said a familiar voice.

Bobbie turned to the man. It was Detective Nolan. She looked away again, unsure of what to say. Finally, it occurred to her that an apology was in order.

'I'm sorry, Detective Nolan. I really cannot imagine what I was thinking. Last night was a mistake. If I'd thought this would mean trouble for you I would never...'

She left the rest of the sentence unsaid and turned once more to Nolan. He nodded to her that the apology was accepted. For the next few moments nothing was said. Then Nolan spoke finally.

'You've come to see Miss Montez?'

Bobbie nodded. She sighed a little and felt tears begin to sting her eyes.

'I'm sorry. Following you was a low trick. I didn't want to put you in trouble again.' This was greeted with a grim smile from the detective. Bobbie's hands were gripping each other so tightly that Nolan could see the fingers turn red in the bitter cold. He stood up. Bobbie followed him with her eyes.

'We can't be seen together again,' he said. There was more than a trace of sadness in his voice. Bobbie nodded but could not trust herself to speak. They looked at one another for a few more moments and then Nolan turned towards the exit. Just before he departed, he glanced back at Bobbie and said, 'Ask her about the War.' Then he turned and walked towards the exit of the park before Bobbie could reply.

She watched him all the way to the car. Her breathing was laboured as she fought to stay in control of her emotions. Finally, she rose from the seat and headed towards the park's exit.

The police car was gone so she felt free to see Miss Montez. The only question, in Bobbie's mind, was would she want to see her? She took the stairs up to the third floor. The building was not so bad as some she had seen. She did not feel unsafe as she might have, for example, if she had been in the tenement where Violet's original family had lived.

She arrived outside Lucia Montez's door. Taking a deep breath, she waited a moment and then knocked.

'Who is it?' came a female voice from inside.

'Hello, Miss Montez, my name is Roberta Flynn. I work for the newspaper, the *New York American*. I was hoping you could help me in the obituary I am writing for Mr George Rankin.'

A white lie, as the article had already been written. Bobbie was becoming more accustomed to mild, in her view, deception, as she pursued a story. From time to time, she did pause and wonder if she was losing something of herself in this headlong pursuit towards the crime desk.

'Obituary?' came the same voice.

Moments later, the door opened a few inches and dark eyes looked out at Bobbie, standing alone in the corridor. One advantage of being five feet three, almost and slender and pretty, is that you are unlikely to strike fear into many people. There was nothing about Bobbie that looked remotely threatening to Lucia Montez. The door opened.

Lucia Montez looked to be around thirty, with large dark eyes limpid enough to drive most sensible men from calm disinterest to marriage proposal, without pausing at the red light. She was quite tall, a little thin, but the old dress she was wearing could not have hung more perfectly on her than if it had been designed by the new French designer, Coco Chanel.

'May I come in Miss Montez?' asked Bobbie. Her voice was also a decided advantage in these situations. Although from New York, Bobbie had been privately schooled at the Gardner School for Girls. She had excelled there and had performed drama regularly. It meant that she spoke with perfect diction and might even have passed for being English, much to her father's dismay. But her mother's influence had always held sway in these matters and Flynn, like most men, just had to do as he was told.

There was a flicker of doubt in the singer's eyes, so Bobbie pressed a little more, 'I know that you were friends with Mr Rankin and it would be a wonderful tribute to him if we could tell our readers just what sort of a person he was.'

'I didn't realise he was so famous.'

He wasn't, of course, but Bobbie was ready for this.

'We like to provide stories about men and women who are not necessarily famous, but who led interesting lives. I know Mr Rankin fought for his country. He was a well-respected musician and his work, with music publishers, meant that many great songs we hear today might very well have been given their chance because of what he did.'

Perhaps it was laying it on a bit thick, but the only thing a young woman liked, more than flattery towards herself, was the indirect flattery of hearing good things spoken about a man who had been in love with her.

'Come in, I've just made some coffee,' said Miss Montez, turning away and gesturing for Bobbie to enter.

The apartment was about the size of a shoebox. There was only one room, although the bed was curtained off from a sofa and a small dining table that was large enough to fit two children. Bobbie smiled hopefully at Miss Montez. The singer rolled her eyes and said, 'Be it ever so humble.' There was a dry humour to the young woman and Bobbie could not help but chuckle at what she'd said. Even Miss Montez smiled. She went over to a coffee pot and poured some coffee into a cup.

'I don't have no sugar or cream.'

'Black is fine,' replied Bobbie, taking the cup from Miss Montez and sitting down on the sofa.

'First of all, I'm sorry for your loss, Miss Montez. I met with some of his band mates from the Ostrich Club, one of them mentioned you were close.'

This brought a half smile from the singer. She replied, 'Yeah, I suppose we were close for a while. You know how it is.' Then Miss Montez sized Bobbie up, in a moment, before adding, with a hint of cynicism, 'Perhaps not, dear. Maybe you don't.'

Bobbie certainly did not want to discuss herself, never mind her love life, such as it was.

'Can you tell me about Mr Rankin. I don't suppose he ever mentioned the War much with you?'

Miss Montez shook her head.

'No, not really. I met him after he came back. I think it affected him badly. He lost a lot of friends, you know. He didn't talk much about it. There was one guy I met who had been with him over there. Then he died and George changed. It was like...I don't know. He just became sad. Like the type of sadness that don't hear no words, that don't need love or company. I don't know. He just changed.'

'May I ask the name of the man who passed away?'

'He was murdered, Miss Flynn. Well, according to George anyway. The police don't think so.'

This piece of news was said in quiet shock. Bobbie's mouth almost fell open. Miss Montez almost smiled at the astonishment on Bobbie's face.

'How terrible,' said Bobbie, for wont of anything better to say.

'I know,' agreed Miss Montez, almost in tears. 'I didn't know him, but it meant a lot to George. He said it was the last of them.'

'The last of them? What did he mean?'

'It was a group of guys he was serving with. They were all musicians. They played concerts for the men. The army gave them instruments and allowed them to entertain behind the lines. Then one day they all got taken out, or at least three of them did. Only George and his friend made it through.'

'What was his friend's name?' asked Bobbie.

'Matt Nicholls. I never met the guy. He and George didn't see each other so much,' Miss Montez paused for a moment before adding, 'He lived in Yonkers.'

This was the name that Detective Nolan had mentioned last night. So, Nicholls and Rankin had both been in France, serving.

'When was he murdered?' asked Bobbie.

'Late November, I think. After that, George was pretty down. I think he was even scared for a while. Him and me drifted apart. He didn't want to see anyone for a while. He didn't want to see me. Then when he decided that he did, I said no.'

At this point Miss Montez broke down. Bobbie put her arm around her and tried to comfort her.

'I'm sorry,' said Bobbie. 'I didn't want to remind you of the pain.'

'It's OK Miss Flynn. I had some cops here earlier. I'm glad people want to know what happened; you know? I don't want him to die and no one gets to answer for it. He was a good guy, George. He didn't hurt no one. Why would someone do that Miss Flynn? Why would someone want to hurt him?'

Bobbie had no answer for the young woman. What could she say? It was a stupid, unforgivable act that had ended a life that had, probably, lived and died many times already. It was a senseless crime, but someone had needed that it happen. Why? What did George Rankin and Matt Nicholls know that meant neither could live.

The answer almost certainly lay in something that had happened four years earlier in another country. How on earth could she find out more about the men that had died? Was such information available from the military? Who could she possibly speak to?

Just then Bobbie felt as lost as the young woman who was crying softly on her shoulder. We lie to ourselves, often, thought Bobbie. We believe and we hope, despite the evidence before our eyes. Reality does not lie, though. It is cold, merciless and true. Bobbie could see no way forward from this point. Not without help. And yet the only help she could think of came in the form of a six-foot detective who had probably been told, by her own father, that he risked his career if he involved Bobbie again in any investigation. This was the reality of her situation.

Reality has one master though: fate. Reality is what is. Fate is something that could be. We just don't know.

And Bobbie was about to find out that fate was prepared to throw out one thread for her to pull on.

12

Tribune Building, New York: 25th January 1922

For the next day, Bobbie buried herself in her work, on the Obituary desk. It was as if the anger, towards her own inability to make progress on investigating the Rankin murder, was propelling her in a direction, at least, to achieving something notable. At the end of the day, she had typed up reams of notes that were generic enough to be used in two dozen obituaries of business and financial notables. Despite himself, Buckner Fanley was impressed. In fact, he was more than impressed, he was worried.

'Miss Flynn,' he said, holding what felt like a volume of War and Peace. 'I have no right to ask you, but is everything all right?'

Bobbie was surprised, rather than affronted, by the question.

'Is there something wrong with the notes?'

'No, Miss Flynn they are,' said Fanley, pausing to find a way to mitigate any hint of praise emanating from his lips, 'quite thorough.'

This brought a half smile to Bobbie's lips. It was clear the old curmudgeon was delighted with her work. Obviously, this satisfaction was well-disguised by the eyes that always seemed full to the brim with imminent doom, as they gazed over the half-moon spectacles. His reluctance, or inability, to dish out praise made Bobbie feel sorry for him rather than angry.

However bad she was feeling, and she was not particularly chipper at that moment, at least she had an appreciation of the good fortune that life had, mostly, bestowed upon her. She had ambition, albeit one that seemed further away than ever before and she had the youthful vigour, combined with no small intelligence, to fight the good fight towards its attainment.

'I'm fine, Mr Fanley. But thank you for asking. I shall see you tomorrow. Cheerio.'

Back at the house, Bobbie rushed to get changed and ready for her night out. This time it was not to be an escapade in the manner that had so spectacularly exploded in both her face and Nolan's too. She came rushing down the stairs to find her father arriving back from work. He took one look at his daughter who was dressed in an understated yet elegant dark dress with, as ever, just enough make up to enhance, but not so much that you would notice.

He looked at her, suspiciously, which brought a forgiving grin from his daughter.

'Don't worry, I'm not with that handsome protégé of yours,' said Bobbie, unable to resist twisting the knife a little.

'Handsome, is he?'

'Violet thinks so,' said Bobbie, warming to her theme. Flynn's brow furrowed.

'Do you, young lady?'

'Well...' replied Bobbie, which said everything, without saying anything.

'Where are you off to tonight?' asked Flynn. Oddly, he trusted Bobbie, notwithstanding what had happened. He knew that she was not about to go off with Nolan again, despite her obvious attempts to provoke him.

'I'm seeing Mary Aston and Lady Frost. They are returning to England in two weeks and they suggested dinner. I gather Kit and his uncle were off playing golf today.'

'Golfers?' said Flynn, in surprise. He was passionate about the game himself but rarely broke one hundred. Like many who played golf, those twin imposters, ambition and addiction, held sway over any evident ability.

'I'll find out if they have any other games planned. Maybe you could join them this weekend,' suggested Bobbie.

He was happy to clutch the peace offering from his daughter, after what had been a depressingly frosty, couple of days since he'd told her off about seeing Nolan. Of course, despite his intentions being for the best, both for her and the young man in question, the reprimand had hurt him much more deeply than his daughter. That was for him to bear. And he would have given anything not to say what he had said, yet nothing would have stopped him from doing so.

He was a father. It was his job.

'Say hello for me,' said Flynn, sketching a smile.

'I will,' said Bobbie, heading out of the door.

Bobbie met her two English friends outside the restaurant, as the two cabs drew up at the same time. Bobbie was immediately greeted by a hug from Mary Aston. They were of a similar age and could both turn a man's head from two hundred paces. The third lady, Lady Agatha Frost, was a septuagenarian whose once slender frame had given way to her enjoyment of the good things in life. Her late husband, Eustace 'Useless' Frost, had committed the unforgivable sin of never having gained weight despite his gargantuan enjoyment of firewater in any form.

After kissing Agatha on both cheeks, the ladies made their way into the French restaurant, *Barbares Américains.* Agatha glanced at the name and then over towards her two companions.

'The owner seems to have a rather poor opinion of his adopted country.'

'He's notoriously rude,' said Bobbie, 'but the food is divine. Daddy and I love to come here, just to watch him being offensive to the customers.'

'Does your father take a notebook with him?' asked Agatha, but there was a twinkle in her eye as she said this.

Bobbie laughed at this and felt all her worries slip away in a moment. It felt good to be with this unusual pair whom she had first met on New Year's Eve when they had helped solve the murder of a fellow journalist on her newspaper, Amory Beaufort.

They were brought to their seats, with Agatha commenting wryly about how every man in the restaurant had seemed to stop eating as the two younger ladies slalomed through the tables to their reserved seats.

'That's Monsieur Bonnard,' said Bobbie as they glanced through their menus. The three ladies eyes went straight to a diminutive Frenchman who was standing with his hands on his hips, legs shoulder width apart, in the manner of a belligerent

Bichon Frisé. His white hair stood up in shock as if in reaction to any implied criticism of his food. The guests, upon whom his death stare was fixed, looked as if they wanted the ground to open up and hide them away.

'Looks a real charmer,' giggled Mary. Then her eyes narrowed, her hand supported her chin and she said, 'Now tell us about this case you solved.'

She was referring to the recovery of Violet Belmont from the most inept kidnappers in the history of this ignoble enterprise.

The story filled the first twenty minutes as they ordered their food and soft drinks arrived. At the end of the story the two English ladies clapped Bobbie for her enterprise and intuition. The next question from Mary was as unavoidably inevitable as it was, also, going to cause her acute embarrassment.

'So how was it to work with Detective Nolan again?' asked Mary. They had also met the detective on New Year's Eve.

'He was surprisingly open to my suggestions,' said Bobbie, evasively. This caused a derisive laugh from Mary and a *sotto voce* comment from Agatha.

'I'll bet he was.'

There was nothing in there for Bobbie to comment on, so she didn't.

'He's rather good-looking,' pointed out Agatha.

This made Mary erupt onto giggles and she admonished her aunt half-heartedly, 'Aunt Agatha!'

'I might be in my seventies, but I'm not entirely blind, you know,' said Agatha without a trace of guilt.

'So, things are going well between you,' suggested Mary. 'How well exactly?'

Silence.

Bobbie looked at the two ladies. The collective intensity of their glare was like a thirty-foot wave rising over you, about to crash down. Bobbie decided that the current approach was never going to work. She decided to embrace full disclosure on the case she was working. It occurred to her that they might even be able to suggest a way forward.

As it happened, they did.

Another ten minutes passed in which the only word that came from the lips of either of the English ladies was an amused 'dancing?' Bobbie wasn't sure if she would not regret that admission, but it was out now, so there was nothing to be done but accept the inevitable questions that it would pose.

When Bobbie had finished talking through the details of the case, including her hypothesis around the involvement of the reclusive writer, O. Bonaty, Mary and Agatha exchanged glances.

'First of all, young lady,' began Agatha, 'you are to be congratulated on the progress so far. I would be inclined to trust your instincts on the Bonaty character. Quite why this should be so remains to be seen. It certainly suggests many things, most obviously around blackmail.'

'Why don't we try and go to see the show?' suggested Mary.

'Tickets might be a problem. I gather it's sold out,' pointed out Bobbie.

'I'm sure we can find a way,' said Agatha, enigmatically. 'Yes, I agree. Are you free tomorrow evening?'

'Yes.'

'Do you think your father would like to come?' asked Mary.

Bobbie hesitated. She was caught between wanting her father to meet these uncommon English ladies once more and having the freedom to pursue the investigation further, without reproach.

'Not a wise idea,' suggested Agatha, reading Bobbie's mind.

'Good point,' agreed Mary. This effectively ended any further discussion on how to involve her father, beyond having him play golf with Kit and Alastair on the coming Saturday.

By now the ladies were enjoying their main course, a Bouillabaisse for Agatha and Beef Bourguignon for the other two ladies.

'Uh oh, French invader at three o'clock,' said Mary. The other two ladies looked up to see the owner of the restaurant with his eyes on them and heading in their direction.

'I would pay good money to see you take him on, Lady Frost,' said Bobbie with a grin.

'The day when jousting with the French ceases to be fun, then it's time I shuffled off this mortal coil,' murmured Agatha.

The little Frenchman arrived looking very pleased with himself and expecting everyone to bask in the afterglow of his Gallic charm.

'I trust the meal is to your satisfaction,' said the Frenchman, puffing out his chest in expectation of the praise he was due.

'Excellent,' chorused Mary and Bobbie. Both eyed each other and then sat back to enjoy the show.

'I see you have a Bouillabaisse, Madame. Our chef is from Marseilles.'

'Is he?' asked Agatha, doubtfully.

'How do you mean?' asked the Frenchman. His face was turning red and the first signs of smoke were beginning to appear from his ears. It was always possible that he might spontaneously combust himself but Agatha, after six decades of needling the French, whom she actually adored, decided to throw a little oil on the fire.

'Don't get me wrong; it's a fine Bouillabaisse. I just wonder why your chef has not perfumed the soup with sea urchins. It's still good. Rather disappointing though.'

The sea urchins had not been delivered that day. That someone should notice was as astonishing as it was rather awkward. It seemed to Monsieur Bonnard that the whole restaurant had ceased to eat, for that moment, and was now in thrall to the confrontation.

Bonnard drew himself up to his full five foot four, puffed out his chest even more, stroked his grey moustache and was about to launch into a force ten Gallic gale when Agatha held one finger up. Now this had the unfortunate effect of both infuriating the Frenchman as well as doing its job and stopping him in his tracks.

'*Nous savons tous les deux que j'ai raison, Monsieur Bonnard. Maintenant, ne faites pas de scandale et ne soyez pas aussi tyrannique à l'avenir, c'est un homme bien,*' said Agatha with a perfect Provencal accent. 'We both know I am right, Mr Bonnard. Now don't make a scene and don't be such a bully in future, there's a good man.'

The Frenchman's eyes widened as his chest deflated like a balloon. He spun around and departed from the ladies *très rapidement,* like a French infantryman at Sedan. Agatha, who was not without a certain amount of vanity, acknowledged the silent acclamation of the diners with a regal nod. The food was exquisite, but Monsieur Bonnard had needed taking down a peg, or three.

Once the excitement had died down, Mary leaned towards Bobbie and said, 'I think we may have a solution for your problem on identifying the soldiers who were in this band with Mr Rankin. Or, at least, who he was serving with that died.'

'How on earth can you gain access to his service record?'

'We have a friend who is rather well-positioned to conduct such inquiries,' replied Mary.

13

Ministry of Defence, Whitehall, London: 25ᵗʰ January 1922

Charles 'Chubby' Chadderton strolled into his Whitehall office, on the stroke of nine in the morning. Sitting outside the office was his secretary of five years, Miss Brooks and another gentleman. The gentleman in question was a youngish man of around twenty-four, who, like Chubby, had suffered an injury during the War. In Chubby's case, it was a result of an encounter that had saved the men under his command. The action had been done, quite literally single-handedly, for Chubby had lost his left-hand courtesy of a German grenade. The young man was missing one leg. His name was John Fenway.

Thanks to the rather odd mindset encouraged at most English Public schools, the tall, very slender Mr Chadderton was known to all as Chubby and the one-legged Mr Fenway was called, Long John.

Miss Brooks received a nod from Chubby, as he walked into the office. She nodded back. Quite why they bothered maintaining any semblance of distance was beyond everyone's guess. Every man and his dog in Whitehall knew that after several years of being in a perfectly professional relationship, matters had taken a turn the previous year and the two were now sweethearts, of a most ardent nature. In fact, they had only parted company from one another thirty minutes previously, after Miss Brooks had spent yet another evening at Chubby's flat. His friends were already betting on when he would be joining Kit, 'Chips' Fry and, rather surprisingly, 'Two Bob' Taylor, in the marriage game.

'There are a number of telegrams for you from America, Mr Chadderton,' said Miss Brooks, in a tone of voice that might have had a monk covering his ears and sprinting to confession.

'From Kit?'

'No Mrs Aston and Lady Frost.'

'Oh,' said Chubby. Just the words "Lady Frost" alone, were enough to make any chap quicken his step. In fact, there were barely two words in Chubby's lexicon, more likely to ensure urgency than "Lady Frost". Agatha, while universally loved by all, was also feared in equal measure. Her tongue was sharper than a Samurai's sword and she could identify a chink in armour from another country.

Sure enough, he spied the two envelopes sitting on his desk. He tore open the first. It was quite a long telegram and it was from Mary. It explained they were helping on a case and that they needed as much information as possible about two American infantry soldiers named George Rankin and Matthew Nicholls, as well as other members of their platoon.

Chubby's role at the Ministry had been created soon after he returned from France. Despite his protests, he was consigned to a desk role at the Ministry dealing with the service records of those who had served in the War and, following its end, their demobilisation.

The telegram briefly explained the situation in New York and the need to gain service records for George Rankin and Matt Nicholls. Having digested what would be needed from Mary's telegram, he tore open the second. This was the one from Kit's Aunt Agatha. It had one line:

AND ASK THAT YOUNG WOMAN TO MARRY YOU

This was typically blunt from Aunt Agatha and it made Chubby smile fondly. Then a thought struck him. The only way that Miss Brooks could have known who the telegrams were from was if she had read them herself. This was not unusual; she often screened such communications. However, it meant she knew what had been said.

Chubby popped his head through the door. Miss Brooks and Long John looked up eagerly.

'Long John,' said Chubby, handing over the telegram, 'be a good chap and get in touch with the cousins. We need this information pronto. I want to know who was in the platoon. I want to know what happened to them. If they were killed, where. If they survived, where are they now? If they went to hospital, where, when? All the usual stuff. Drop everything else. This is urgent.'

Long John took the telegram and immediately left the office. He had only just recently stopped saluting Chubby, at the latter's request.

After he had left the office, Chubby looked down at the second telegram. Miss Brooks was no longer looking at Chubby but was rearranging a few stray pencils that had moved a quarter of an inch from their usual place. She continued to ignore him as he moved towards her. Even as his arms encircled her head and his face came down bedside her, she was most assiduous in ensuring her full attention was devoted to the arrangements on her desk. Her professional detachment lasted only until she heard Chubby whisper something in her ear.

'I shall, you know. And sooner than you think.'

14

Jackson Theatre, New York: 26th January 1922

Owing to a previous engagement, Mary and Agatha were unable to meet Bobbie until seven o'clock. They saw one another outside the theatre, which was hosting, according to the poster featuring a girl with very long legs and a very short skirt, an extended run of *Heaven's Below*.

After they had greeted one another, Bobbie said excitedly, 'Well I don't know how you managed to find the tickets but well done.'

Mary smiled back to Bobbie, 'Sometimes one has to pull rank.' She glanced towards Agatha and added, 'Having a member of the British nobility attend a show is never bad for publicity. We just agreed to be interviewed, about the show, by the theatre manager, Mr Moss, and our comments to be used for publicity purposes.'

Bobbie laughed delightedly at this. Then her face became more serious, 'Any news from your friend on Mr Rankin and Mr Nicholls?'

'Not yet. Chubby said it might take a couple of days, but he's as good as his word. He'll find the service records. You can count on him.'

'Thank you, Mary,' said Bobbie and then she turned around to look for Agatha. 'Where's...?'

The crowds were brushing past them as they surged towards the entrance. However, there was an island of serenity as Agatha studied the playbill outside the theatre. She seemed fascinated, or shocked, by the state of dress, or undress, of the young woman.

Bobbie and Mary wandered over to her and stood before the playbill.

'She seems a little under-dressed,' observed Agatha. The name of the show was emblazoned in bold, bright red letters. The name of the producer, Herman Moss, was just above, proudly presenting the book by Omar Maltbie III and songs by O. Bonaty.

'Shall we go in?' said Bobbie. 'Where are we sitting exactly?'

In England, it would have been described as the Royal Box. Bobbie couldn't believe it when they arrived at their seats in the first box to the right of the circle.

'I've never sat here before,' she exclaimed.

'The young lady I spoke to insisted,' said Agatha matter-of-factly. 'I hope the show matches the view.'

The three ladies were engrossed by the show, even though it appeared to have little by way of a plot, character development or, indeed, any narrative worthy of the name. Instead, it seemed a collection of scenes, glued together by songs in search of a point that they never quite located.

The songs, however, were certainly pleasant, from the point of view of their melody, but after a while, the lack of lyrical depth and the same 32-bar pattern began to wear. Perhaps, the fatigue was as much due to the fact that the ladies were listening intently to the words hoping to find some clue as to their mysterious creator, or even any connection to the murders. On both counts, their hopes were dashed. The songs were light and certainly hummable. Bobbie could see why they had made an impression on the music publisher.

The end of the show brought one encore, from the one unequivocal bright spot of the evening, the song and dance lead, Miss Janice Griffith. She carried the show with her bright patter, virtuoso dancing and a delicate light soprano voice that made a perfect foil for the simple melodies and unsophisticated lyrics. This, perhaps, was the essence of the show's success. The combination of a new star performer and a series of songs that demanded little of the listener.

The three ladies agreed that the show had passed pleasantly enough, without ever pausing to take up space in their collective memory. As the curtain came down, the lights went up. The ladies rose from their seats just as there was a knock at the door of their box.

Mary was nearest the door. She opened it to reveal a very plump man in his fifties, perspiring as if he had been running through Death Valley in summer.

'Have I the pleasure of addressing Lady Agatha Frost,' he said looking at the vision that was Mary Aston.

'That would be me,' said Agatha, stepping forward briskly. She ignored the man's face falling. It had been over thirty years since she turned men's heads. It wasn't something she missed particularly. The younger generation of women were, perhaps, going to be a little more susceptible to disappointment, in her view. Society's increasing scrutiny of women's faces and bodies, on stage and screen, bordered on objectification. Agatha doubted the situation would improve much, until women became more autonomous. They barely had the vote.

'Lady Frost,' said the man, pushing out his hand, for wont of any other method of greeting Agatha.

For once Agatha took pity on the poor man and consented to shake his hand.

'Would you be Mr Moss?' asked Agatha, shrewdly.

'The very same, Lady Frost, the very same. And may I ask who your delightful young companions are?' asked Moss.

Bobbie and Mary stepped out of the room and shook Moss's hand.

'This is my niece, Mrs Mary Aston. She has come over from England with me. And this is Miss Bobbie Flynn, who is a leading journalist on the *New York American*.' Agatha accompanied this with a slight wink towards Bobbie that was unseen by the impresario.

Bobbie had to cover her mouth at Agatha's rather embellished view of her status in the newspaper.

'Would you like to meet Miss Griffith?' suggested Moss. 'I think she would be thrilled to meet real life English nobility.'

'That would be marvellous,' said Agatha.

They chatted for a few minutes more, to allow the audience to leave the theatre and then Moss led them downstairs and through the auditorium, up onto the stage, via some stairs, which bypassed the orchestra pit. Many of the orchestra were still there, packing up, chatting or smoking. They followed Moss up onto the stage and then behind the curtain, which took them backstage.

It was fascinating to see the sets from the other side of the curtain. He led them past some Chesterfield chairs and bookcases, which were used in a song set in a country house.

There was also an old western saloon. Why the female lead ended up in these various locales was quite beyond the ladies and it was not something they intended asking, when they met Miss Griffith.

The dressing rooms of the performers were down another set of stairs at the side of the stage. Soon they were outside a door with a star, inside of which was written the name Miss J Griffith.

'Here we are,' said Moss. He rapped the door and asked, 'Say Janice my dear, are you ready for your visitors?'

'Sure,' said a voice from inside. The accent was more distinctly New York than her stage voice.

They entered the dressing room, which was a little smaller than Bobbie had imagined it would be. There was a small sofa, a wardrobe and dressing table with a mirror, fringed with lights, before which, Miss Griffith sat. She turned around and smiled a greeting to the visitors.

'Janice, this is Lady Frost, Mrs Aston and Miss Flynn. Mrs Aston is married to a real-life lord and Miss Flynn is a journalist on the *New York American.*'

'Say, you girls could be on stage too,' said Miss Griffith eyeing Bobbie and Mary.

'My niece has been known to tread the boards,' said Agatha drily. The only times she'd seen this were when they were on a case that led them to a shady nightclub outside San Francisco and on a case involving murder at a theatre.

'Congratulations, Miss Griffith,' said Bobbie. 'We loved the show.'

'Call me Janice,' said Miss Griffith, grinning at the praise. 'I love the show. I'm the luckiest girl (*she said goil*) in New York.'

'How did you get the role?' asked Agatha.

Moss replied on behalf of Miss Griffith.

'It was the song writer who suggested we speak to Janice. We went to see her at a nightclub in Queens and we were knocked out.'

Bobbie turned to Miss Griffith, 'So you know the mysterious Mr Bonaty?'

'No, I've never met him. I guess he saw me one night and suggested me to Mr Moss. Lucky break for me, huh?'

'It certainly was,' replied Agatha, trying to hide her disappointment.

'So how did you come to use Mr Bonaty's songs, Mr Moss?' asked Mary.

'I was putting on a show and I wanted some songs. I sent word to a few music publishers about what I wanted. I said I wanted someone new. I didn't want someone like Berlin, or Kern and Wodehouse or those Gershwin boys. New blood, that's what I wanted. So, the music publishers sent down some song pluggers, to play me some of their work. Bonaty stood out, no question.'

'And you've never met him?' asked Bobbie.

'No, we always work through his lawyer, Ben Strauss. No one ever sees him. I tried, but he refused. We were almost going to can the songs and get someone else in but we liked the work and decided maybe we could use this recluse thing. I am sure glad we did.'

'I'll bet,' said Bobbie smiling at the producer. 'You have a great show and a wonderful star to perform these lovely songs.'

Bobbie ignored the glance from Agatha, which she took to be a warning not to lay it on too thick. However, in this,

Agatha was wrong and Bobbie knew her market well. Americans like praise the way whales like plankton: dispensed in large quantities.

'That's so kind of you Miss Flynn,' said Miss Griffith.

'I'm sure you must owe a debt of gratitude to the song plugger who brought you those wonderful songs.'

'Yes, we sure do. I said to Sol, if you ever want a job with us, you just must ask. And you know what? He did.'

'Sol?' asked Bobbie.

'Sol Maxim. He's our pianist on the orchestra. Great guy. Would you like to meet him? I'm sure he's still around. Besides which, I think we should let Janice change now.'

'Oh, don't worry about me,' said Miss Griffith, who was still entranced at the idea of being with the next best thing to royalty. She was dying to know if the English ladies had met the king.

The idea of meeting the man who had been the original song plugger for Bonaty was too strong, however. Bobbie and her two companions made their excuses and allowed Moss to take them to the orchestra pit.

They retraced their footsteps down the corridor but diverted away from the stairs leading up to the stage and, instead, went underneath. Soon they were in the orchestra pit. Many of the musicians had departed, but luckily the man they wished to speak to remained.

Sol Maxim was about as tall as Agatha which is to say not very. He was in his mid-thirties with short, slicked back hair and pencil-thin moustache. He looked up hopefully as he saw the two young women approach with Moss.

'Hey Sol,' began Moss, 'Some ladies want to meet the man who met Bonaty.'

'I wish I had,' laughed Sol.

'Have you ever heard from him?' asked Bobbie, soon after Moss had made the introductions.

'No. I only ever dealt with Mr Strauss. I knew him from another client of his, from a few years back. He approached with some handwritten sheet music and lyrics and asked me what I thought. I played the songs and said they were good. Very good, in fact. He asked me if I would show them to Mr Feist and I said I would be delighted. You never know, I always say.'

'How did Mr Strauss get hold of the songs?'

'He told me they just arrived in the mail. Can you believe that?' said Sol shaking his head in a you-never-can-tell manner.

'Say, Miss Flynn, are you going to write a story about this?' suggested Moss hopefully. There was nothing better than free publicity through the press. Anything that kept the hubbub around Bonaty's true identity was always likely to keep the cash tills ringing.

'It's a thought,' grinned Bobbie. 'You know, it's definitely a thought.'

'May I ask a question?' asked Mary.

'Shoot,' said Sol, disconcertingly.

'I'll try not to wound,' smiled Mary. 'Do you still have the original sheet music?'

Sol's smile widened.

'Do you know, I might have forgotten to hand one of the songs back.'

16

Lindy's, New York: 27th January 1922

Another morning passed with no news from Chubby. Mary and Agatha met Bobbie for lunch, in the early afternoon, at Lindy's to discuss the next steps in their investigation. The two English ladies only had a week and a half left before they were due to sail back to Europe. Bobbie very much considered them as co-conspirators and they certainly viewed themselves in this way, too.

Whether it was the lack of news from the police side of the investigation or impatience at having to wait for information that might never come, but Bobbie was at a low ebb in the restaurant.

'I feel we are rapidly approaching another dead end,' she confessed. 'Are you sure that your friend can come up with the goods?'

The two ladies tried to reassure her that Chubby would come through for them. Bobbie was less certain. It always seemed like an outside chance, that he would be able to find such specific information, never mind have the U.S. Army hand it over to him.

Agatha's patience was limited at the best of times and she, like Bobbie, was hankering to get some momentum on the case. She leaned forward into the group, always a sign that one should listen, and shared some of her thoughts.

'I think you should keep your chin up young lady. I think we are making progress but I admit, it's rather difficult to pinpoint what that is exactly. I think your hunch around this Bonaty character is correct. That's why I am going to propose we quickly finish our lunch and make a call on his lawyer, Mr Strauss, to find out more.'

'Will he see us?' wondered Bobbie out loud.

'I think you'll find that having "Lady" before your name opens more doors than it closes, even in the colonies,' observed Agatha, drily.

This brought a chuckle from Bobbie, who felt her mood lightening already. Mary and Agatha were a real tonic, in the absence of being able to share her ideas with a certain detective in the Midtown North precinct. Still, she would give the world to know how his investigation was proceeding.

'Well, I'm game if you are,' said Bobbie.

Then, Mary added another thought to their plan for the day. She said, 'I was also thinking that if you have been debarred from seeing Detective Nolan, there's nothing to stop Aunt Agatha and myself paying a visit and, you know, hearing about his progress.'

Bobbie's smile widened at this, although another part of her felt empty at the thought of not joining them.

'Good idea, Mary. He will certainly make time to see us,' replied Agatha. 'And I'm equally convinced he'll be interested to hear about how our inquiries are proceeding.'

'I'm sure he'd rather hear it from you, Bobbie' grinned Mary. Bobbie coloured at this, but said nothing to confirm or, indeed, deny that this would be so.

The offices of Ben Strauss & Co were on 29th Street near 6th Avenue. The ladies alighted from the cab and stood before the office. 'I suppose this is it,' said Agatha, rather unimpressed by the old building. 'I hope it doesn't fall down while we're inside.'

They entered the building and climbed the stairs to the first floor to the lawyer's office. The office had a rather anonymous exterior, consisting of just a heavy oak door with a small, brass nameplate – Ben Strauss & Co.

Bobbie went forward and knocked on the door. They waited for a few seconds and then it was answered by a woman of around thirty.

'May I help you?'

Bobbie answered for the ladies. 'We would like to see Mr Strauss if he is available.'

The lady beckoned for them to come in. They found themselves in a room with a desk, presumably used by the lady who had greeted them.

The walls, rather like the offices of Leo Feist, were covered with photographs of Broadway stars, many with a man who the ladies presumed to be Strauss and sheet music artwork. The impression, whether true or not, was of a man who was very well connected in the theatre world.

'May I ask your names and why you wish to see Mr Strauss.'

Agatha decided it was time to play her ace.

'I am Lady Agatha Frost, this is Mrs Mary Aston and Miss Roberta Flynn,' said Agatha. She had adopted to use Bobbie's full name, following a conversation in the taxi.

The secretary disappeared into an office before returning two minutes later, with a warmer smile.

'Please come in. Mr Strauss can see you now.'

The ladies trooped into the office that was generous in size with not one but two leather sofas either side of a coffee table. There was also a cocktail cabinet that did not try to hide its illicit stock. As with the outer office, the room was bedecked by photographs and theatrical posters, aside from one wall that was set aside for a floor-to-ceiling bookcase containing legal tomes.

Strauss was on his feet immediately and over to the ladies. He was younger and better-looking than he seemed in the photographs. Bobbie would have put his age at around thirty to thirty-five. His hair was dark and his eyes darker still, but the smile was wide and warm.

'This is an honour,' said Strauss holding out his hand to Agatha first and then the other two ladies. 'I've never met a real-life lady before.'

'You should get out more,' replied Agatha, stiffly, but there was enough of a twinkle in her eyes to make Strauss laugh. He shook hands with Bobbie and Mary, before gesturing to them to sit on the sofa.

'Now, ladies, how may I help you?'

'We are interested in investing in a show in London. To take place in our West End. It's rather like your Broadway. Lots of theatres.'

'Hey, I know all about your West End. In fact, I met a young man from your country last year who wants to take his plays to Broadway. Noel Coward. Are you familiar with him?'

'Noel,' said Mary, 'how wonderful. He's such a charming man.' Mary was aware of Noel Coward but had not met him.

It was a slight risk to praise him thus, but they were already far out on a limb.

'I'll say. Funniest guy I ever met. He'll go over big here, mark my words. Now, you say you're interested in taking which show to the West End?'

'Perhaps *"Heavens Below"*, it seems to be doing rather well over here,' answered Mary, in a voice that was somewhere between bored and half-interested. She made it seem more like an afterthought than the initial thrust of a negotiation.

Strauss sighed a little and said, 'I will not lie to you, ladies, there is a lot of interest in this piece. It is not just the show. You know, of course, the great mystery surrounding the writer.'

'We'd heard that he is rather reclusive,' said Mary.

'He sure is. I never even met the guy and I am his lawyer. How is that for a deal?' asked Strauss laughing and shaking his head.

'Uncommon,' agreed Agatha. 'So, you say you have never actually met Mr Bonaty.'

'Never. I just receive letters and then I send him cheques marked 'Cash'. Mr Bonaty sure doesn't want anyone to know who he is. The strange thing is, the more he hides from public view, the more people want to know about him.'

'How is it possible to maintain this extraordinary public stance?' asked Mary. 'I would've thought there must be some requirement for him to make an appearance.'

Strauss shook his head and replied, 'There isn't. We deal entirely by mail. We send everything to a mailbox. Out of curiosity, we sent someone to look at who picked up the mail, but he sent along a boy to the box and we lost the child. We decided we wouldn't do that again. He's making us too much money and we don't want to risk upsetting the relationship.'

'Does Mr Bonaty have any other songs to be published.'

'No. He says that this may happen in the future, but he will not give us a date. Trust me, Hermann Moss is all over me about this, so is George Cohan and Mr Ziegfeld. I told Bonaty but he doesn't seem to care.'

'Or perhaps there are no more songs,' murmured Agatha, enigmatically.

This was not picked up by Strauss, but both Bobbie and Mary shot Agatha a look.

'So, what do you have in mind?' asked Strauss, getting down to business. This was the three ladies' cue to leave.

'We shall have to see, Mr Strauss. The arrangement is altogether very uncommon,' said Agatha, doubtfully. 'I shall have to talk with my fellow investors, to let them know of the unusual arrangements. We were rather hoping Mr Bonaty would come to London to help us publicise any opening.'

'I could certainly ask,' said Strauss, hoping not to lose the interest of a potential backer.

'Could you ask if he would be prepared to meet us?' said Agatha. 'We would treat any meeting with the utmost confidentiality, of course. Let me write down my address. If you could send me a telegram on Mr Bonaty's decision, we would be very grateful.'

Agatha wrote down the address that she was staying at in New York and then the three ladies took their leave from the lawyer. They hailed a cab which, with the double attraction of both Bobbie and Mary, almost caused a car crash among a handful of yellow cabs rushing to pick up the fare.

'What do you think, Lady Frost?' asked Bobbie, before instructing the cab to go to the Tribune building.

Agatha's face was inscrutable but this, for once, was only to hide her level of despondency.

'I suspect that we need not hold our breath waiting to meet the mysterious Mr Bonaty this way. It seems to me, anyone so keen to remain anonymous has a jolly good reason to do so.'

'I wonder what that is,' said Bobbie, giving voice to everyone's thoughts on the subject.

17

Detectives Nolan and Yeats sat in an office, alongside Lieutenant Grimm, listening to their, highly un-esteemed captain, Frank O'Riordan's pep talk which consisted of eighty percent criticism and twenty percent threat. The lack of progress on the Rankin murder was beginning to get noticed in high places, specifically the Commissioner, Richard Enright. When that happened, his displeasure was communicated directly to Inspector Flynn and then communicated to O'Riordan. Sometimes Inspector Flynn was bypassed, as he was on this occasion and O'Riordan was the happy recipient of a call directly from 240 Centre Street, which housed the office of Enright and his staff.

The call with Enright had lasted barely two minutes and had not permitted O'Riordan much opportunity to rebut the accusations of incompetence in the handling of the case. Part of O'Riordan's issue in dealing with the Commissioner was that Enright had once been a cop himself and risen through the ranks. Pulling wool, or any other item of clothing, over his eyes was next to impossible. Enright's final warning had been ominous.

'If you don't get this solved in two days, I'm handing it over to Midtown South precinct.'

This was the ultimate indignity and O'Riordan knew he would never live it down if this came to pass. His ambitions would be thwarted. City Hall, 240 Centre Street, would all go up in smoke. He would not allow this to happen and he needed someone to blame. Lieutenant Grimm was too new and Yeats was a little too much of a loose cannon. He'd never liked Nolan and had many reasons to want to take him down a little.

He stood over the three men after haranguing them for five minutes on what the Commissioner had said. Then he leaned over and fixed his eyes on them one by one.

'Now, what do you intend doing about it?'

The clock struck five as he said this and the sound of the hand hitting the number twelve resounded like a gunshot in the office.

Ever the politician, Grimm decided to up the ante.

'Good question, captain,' said Grimm turning towards the two young detectives and glaring at them.

'Exactly how do you intend bringing this to a resolution? I've been reading your reports and don't get me started on the spelling and grammar...'

O'Riordan had no intention of getting Grimm started on the spelling and grammar, instead he stared at the diminutive lieutenant open-mouthed.

Nolan took it upon himself to become the lightning rod. He cleared his throat and addressed O'Riordan, ignoring his lieutenant entirely.

'We have spoken to everyone in the tenement, including the superintendent. No one saw Rankin come home that night and no one saw anyone leave his apartment. We have a list of the people who entered and left the building that night and morning. All of them check out. It's like the killer was a ghost. The fire escape was bolted from the inside of Rankin's apartment and we both tried to leave through it and shut it behind us. It wouldn't lock. We've spoken to everyone that knew him and he hadn't an enemy in the world. We have no motive; we have no means or opportunity.'

'Then how the hell do you explain the dead body in the room?' said Grimm, leaping in ahead of O'Riordan. It was difficult to say who was more irritated by this – the two young detectives or O'Riordan, who had not intended that the lieutenant slither away from any of the blame. The conversation was slowly slipping away from the captain, so he decided to grab some control back.

'Grimm, I want you over this case now. I want you to take direct control and find me the killer.'

'Would that be within two days, sir?' asked Nolan, knowing that this was anathema to the lieutenant. He ignored the molten lava pouring from Grimm's eyes. There would be a price to pay for his comment, but he was past caring.

'Yes, two days Grimm, do you hear?'

'Yes, sir,' said Grimm trying to sound enthusiastic.

O'Riordan departed at this point and left Grimm with the two detectives. Grimm turned his full fury on Nolan, but it was cold in nature, calm and precise, which made it all the more deadly.

'Nolan, I want the case file up to date and on my desk at eight o'clock tomorrow morning. I don't care if you are here all night writing up statements. Is this clear?'

'Yes sir,' replied Nolan.

'Yeats,' continued Grimm, 'you and I will visit all the people who spoke to you in the building. Someone saw something. No one can just enter and leave a building unseen. No one. You've missed something and I intend finding out just what.'

Nolan sat down at his desk and began the laborious task of writing up the statements from the morning and early afternoon. Yeats dropped down beside him and clapped him on the back.

'You dumb mutt, what were you thinking, making a crack like that,' said Yeats laughing. He then imitated Nolan saying, 'Would that be within two days, sir?'

Even Nolan was laughing now. He shook his head ruefully and smiled at his partner. He said, 'Yeah, it was pretty stupid, but did you see the look on Grimm's face.'

Yeats fought to stop himself erupting in laughter. The two men sensed the lieutenant's eyes on them from his office. Yeats made a play at pointing to things on the statement, arrayed before Nolan on his desk. He doubted this was fooling anybody.

After Yeats left for the evening, Nolan began to copy out the statements onto official police forms. While he was doing this, Mulcahy, a patrolman, popped into the squad room.

'Hey Nolan, you have some visitors downstairs.'

Nolan glanced up at Mulcahy and nodded.

'Who?'

'You're not going to believe this,' came the reply.

The rather vague reply from Mulcahy was accompanied only by a smile and no further comment. This forced Nolan to give up his administrative duties, temporarily, to go and see what had amused Mulcahy so.

The sight of Agatha and Mary sitting alongside a rather diverse bunch of individuals in the entrance hall of the precinct provided his answer. Flanking Agatha on one side was 'Lefty' Mulligan who enjoyed modest success as a burglar, despite what one might have considered the rather disadvantageous absence of his right hand.

On Mary's right was a lady whose profession was listed as 'hostess'. She was in a dress that was, at least, three sizes too small to contain a generously proportioned chest. And perhaps this was the point. She and Mary were chatting happily enough, which amused Nolan. He had first met the ladies on a case on New Year's Eve. This was when he had first met the daughter of Inspector Flynn.

Two thoughts immediately struck the young detective as he walked towards the two ladies. Firstly, they were emissaries from the young lady that Inspector Flynn had made clear he was not to see. Nolan wasn't sure how he felt about this, which is to say he was delighted and conflicted, in equal measure.

The second thought that struck him and was no less the subject of an inner conflict, was that the two ladies had inveigled themselves into helping Bobbie on the case. Professional pride naturally rebelled against such a prospect, perhaps even some latent male insecurity, although, to give Nolan his due, he was less prone to this malady than most chaps. There were some potential advantages in their involvement. The mere idea of this was both anathema and welcome. Bobbie, Agatha and Mary had proved themselves very useful at New Year and Bobbie, subsequently, on the Violet Belmont kidnapping. There was no question, Lady Frost had a first-class mind, to go with a tongue that took no prisoners.

In short, Nolan was immensely curious.

'Ladies, this is a pleasure. Perhaps we should find somewhere a little less crowded to speak.'

Agatha and Mary concurred, although they would scarcely have predicted that a police cell would be the location of their meeting, due to the lack of free interview rooms in the precinct.

Agatha looked around her and said, 'It's been a while since I was in a police cell.'

'A regular occurrence Lady Frost?' asked Nolan, amused at the idea, but sceptical.

'More than you might believe,' said Agatha nostalgically, before getting down to business. 'No doubt you will have surmised that we have come at the request of Miss Flynn and that we have been helping her in her inquiries.'

'Yes,' acknowledged Nolan.

'I think the time has come to pool our resources,' said Agatha, continuing her train of thought. 'I imagine that you will be coming under some pressure to make progress on the Rankin murder.'

This was certainly true and the reasons for this would have surprised Nolan. However, he contented himself by asking, 'Have you any information that might be of help to the investigation.'

'Are you prepared to share what you have?' asked Mary.

Nolan was silent for a moment and then said slowly, 'Yes.'

'Good,' said Agatha. 'Since you last saw Miss Flynn outside the house of Miss Montez and kindly tipped her the lead around the War, we have used some sources of our own to find out who Mr Rankin served with that might have some bearing on the case. The information we sought arrived this afternoon.'

This brought a raised eyebrow from Nolan. The US Army had been taking an age to come back to him on this. Nolan took out of his breast pocket, the photograph he had found in the apartment of Rankin showing the dead man with four other uniformed men, all holding musical instruments. He showed it to the two English women.

'Ah,' said Mary. 'Interesting.' She pointed to Rankin and to Matt Nicholls. Agatha nodded sagely and fixed her attention back on Nolan. 'I wish we had seen this sooner. It might have hastened our search. This business of excluding Miss Flynn, from the investigation, is decidedly vexing.'

Nolan was increasingly of the same view.

'Are you aware of who all these men are and what happened to them?' asked Agatha, her eyes remaining on the photograph of the five men.

The look on Nolan's face confirmed that he did not know.

Agatha's mouth moved in a manner that suggested she was about to speak. For a long time. She began, 'Then let us enlighten you. We don't know the full facts, I might add, but we have some pieces of the jigsaw.'

Agatha turned the photograph over. There were five names written down in a spidery handwriting. She read them out.

18

Second Battle of Marne, North-eastern France: 15th July 1918

Mid-morning.

The air around the group of men seemed to vibrate with the din of explosions. There were five of them, huddled inside a shelter dug into the side of the trench. No one looked up, for fear of being blinded by the rock or muck being thrown up around them, or by shrapnel. Or perhaps they did not want the others to see the terror in their eyes.

Each man was thinking the same thing. *Why am I here?*

The question had sometimes been raised, in an oblique way. There was the song Oscar had written. The title had a couple of extra words and would never see the light of day, on any stage, but the men in the platoon enjoyed it. How many of the 38th Infantry had heard it now? Plenty. Even old General McAlexander had heard it by accident. He'd laughed. The men had loved him for that.

Would they ever play it again?

The ground shuddered beneath their feet as the bombardment continued. They'd been attacked before. This was nothing new. What was different was the fact that, in a seemingly absurd moment of concord, the Allies had decided to attack the Germans at the very same moment. Both fronts were under the most extraordinary assault from guns that were miles behind each line.

Rankin opened one fearful eye and wished he hadn't as one poor man disappeared in a cloud of smoke. Perhaps joining the artillery would have been a better idea. He offered a quick prayer to himself, and to the man that was no longer, and pressed himself harder against the trench wall. There were shouts everywhere around him but they were in a losing battle against the screams of the bombs and the outright terror of the men.

Why am I here?

Whistles now. They surely weren't going to attack in this maelstrom. More whistles and shouts.

Apparently, they were.

Madness.

Utter, uninhibited madness.

Rankin stayed pressed against the rock. He noted Oscar, Matt, Archie and Lance were not moving. He wouldn't either. Nothing in this war game for him.

Why am I here?

He could have been at the Lavender Club, playing or singing. What on earth had made this seem like a good idea? He knew though.

Cherchez la femme.

He'd learned that phrase in France, but it explained so much of life. There was no one girl to blame. In fact, it was not as if he could blame the women per se. It was his choice.

Girls love a man in uniform they'd said.

They were right.

And then he'd left for France. Over there, everyone wore a uniform so he was not exactly standing out from the crowd. And demand outstripped supply. Hundreds of thousands of men. Not many girls. They were in hiding and, given the almighty shellacking they were getting at that moment, who could blame them?

Another bomb landed near them, covering the men in gravel. The sound of whistles grew louder. Was Fritz attacking them?

'Hey, Lance, go find out what they want?' shouted Rankin.

This brought a grim laugh from the other men. All of them had their hands over their ears. The heads jerked, spasmodically, with every new shell.

A voice nearby shouted. Rankin looked up. It was the new sergeant. He was out in the middle of the trench, clutching a whistle. He was gesturing to them to leave the shelter. Moments later he wasn't there. Rankin felt like he was going to be ill.

Then all of a sudden, the air seemed to leave their shelter. Rankin couldn't breathe. There was a scream of a shell. An explosion. Then silence.

Two hours later, the medics were going through the trench. The list of men declared dead from the bombardment was growing at an alarming rate. The medics picked their way through the bodies, collecting name tags or calling for a stretcher. It was gruesome work. The sights they encountered would feed a thousand nightmares in the years ahead.

'Over here,' shouted one medic as they arrived at the shelter that had housed, briefly, George Rankin and his four

friends. The medic looked at the carnage. Twisted pieces of metal that looked as if, once upon a time, they had been musical instruments. Three men lay dead on the floor. Two others appeared to be wounded but alive.

'Check out these two guys,' said the medic. 'Maybe we can save them.' Even as he said this, he doubted it. The two men were covered in blood, but they were breathing. One of them was lying beside a leather-bound book. Out of curiosity, the medic opened the book. It was full of handwritten notes and musical notations.

Songs.

He put the book with one of the men still breathing and went to the dead men.

'Stretcher bearer,' shouted the medic. 'Hurry. They may be alive. Take that notebook too. Might be important,' It was a folly to believe they would be. Everyone was exhausted to their bones and sick of war.

He sighed and reached down into the shirt of the first dead man. He turned to his comrade.

'You ready?'

The man nodded.

'Okay. This is Oscar...'

19

Midtown North Precinct, New York: 27th January 1922

'Oscar,' said Agatha looking up at Mary.

'Horowitz,' replied Mary, staring down at a sheaf of papers that had been telegrammed by Chubby earlier that afternoon. 'Oscar Horowitz died 15th July 1918.'

'Archie,' said Agatha, her eyes once more flicking up to Mary from the back of the photograph.

Mary scanned a couple of pieces of paper. Then her eyes widened slightly, 'There was an Archibauld. He died though on the 15th, same day as Oscar Horowitz. Archibauld Wilde'.

Agatha nodded, but there was a look of sadness on her face, noted by the young detective. He felt it himself. The memories, of that awful few months in France, came back to him. So many young lives lost. He felt a hand encircle his and realised Mary had seen his reaction to the grim business they were conducting.

'I'm so sorry,' said Mary.

Nolan nodded but found that he was unable to speak.

'Matt,' read Agatha from the back of the photograph.

It took a few moments to find the name and then Mary read out, 'Matthew Nicholls. Wounded 15th January 1918. He stayed in a hospital for two weeks and then was moved back to

England until September when he returned to the United States. He was demobbed from the army in February 1919.'

'Why did he not return to the War?' asked Agatha.

Mary frowned and looked up, a little reluctantly, at her adopted aunt, 'He'd lost a foot. It says here that the time in England was spent creating a prosthetic foot for him and helping him to walk again.'

Agatha waited until Mary had finished reading then she turned her attention to Nolan.

'Was this Mr Rankin's friend, the one who died in December?'

Nolan nodded, but it was clear he was not happy with what he understood of the case.

'According to the police report, it was suicide. Nicholls had suffered with depression since returning from the War and was drinking heavily. He shot himself.'

'Has the case not been reopened in the light of Mr Rankin's death?'

'No,' replied Nolan, barely able to suppress his anger. He shook his head and suddenly felt tired. The talk of the War was affecting him and the more he tried to hide this fact the more he felt a fatigue that he had not felt since he'd been in France.

Sensing how difficult this was for Nolan, Agatha forged on, believing it was best to get things out of the way.

'Mr Rankin, we know about and that leaves the final member of the group, Lance Graham.'

'Lance Graham,' repeated Mary as her eyes skimmed over the list. Then she found her man. 'Not good news. It seems he died on the 15th of July too. It must have been a terrible day.'

'The opening day of the second Battle of Marne,' said Nolan. His voice was barely a whisper. His eyes glistened with tears. He nodded to the two ladies. 'And yes, it was a terrible day.' Mary's hand gripped Nolan's more tightly and he was grateful.

'Did Mr Rankin end up in a hospital too?' asked Agatha.

Mary glanced once more down at her list.

'Yes, he did. He went to the same mobile field hospital near the front as Matt Nicholls and then they went to Bouleuse to be patched up. Then I think that's where they separated. Mr Nicholls went to England while Mr Rankin ended up in Paris until September when he returned to the fighting until the end of the War. He was demobbed in May 1919.'

Silence followed these remarks from Mary. It was like an unspoken prayer for the fallen. There seemed little else that could be added to their understanding. Nolan made some notes from the telegrams in Mary's possession. He nodded his thanks to the two ladies. Tacitly they decided to end the meeting. They left the cell and walked back down the corridor and up the stairs. Before entering the entrance hallway, Nolan thanked the ladies for their help. However, he finished on a note of cold reality.

'I'm not sure how all this helps us though. I trust Bobbie's instincts on this, but we have nothing that connects his death to what happened that day in 1918.'

'I agree,' said Agatha. 'But you are right to trust that young woman's instincts. I wish her father would too. I think there is something to it. The coincidences are just too overwhelming to ignore. We just must keep batting away and hope that something turns up. Those two young men were murdered.

They were murdered by the same hand. They were murdered because of something that united them that dates back to the War. This is our pole star, Detective Nolan. Do not lose sight of it.'

For the first time in a while, Nolan smiled at the old lady before him. She was without question one of the most unusual people he had ever met. Quite what she must have been like in her youth he could only guess. He glanced towards Mary who was looking at her aunt affectionately. They were very alike in many ways.

'I shall have to leave you ladies now. I have a stack of statements to fill out.'

'Really?' frowned Agatha. 'So late?'

'Captain O'Riordan was in a foul mood earlier. The Commissioner is on his case about the lack of progress. He tore a strip off O'Riordan and Inspector Flynn, I gather. So O'Riordan tore a strip off me. I guess that's fair enough.'

Agatha winced a little as she heard this.

'I'm so sorry,' she said.

'Not your fault,' said Nolan, with a grin. He left them at this point and went back up the stairs. They watched him depart and then Mary turned to Agatha, with one eyebrow raised.

'Not your fault?' asked Mary eyeing her aunt closely.

Agatha looked away and shrugged.

'I did it for the greater good. Detective Nolan and Inspector Flynn are big boys. A telling off won't hurt them.'

Mary laughed at this, 'True, they are big boys, but it was still a little devious.'

'I know, but Eustace used this trick many times and I can report that it worked on every occasion. I see no reason why my calling the Commissioner, to complain about the lack of progress on the case, should not furnish us with ample opportunity to advance the cause of Miss Flynn's involvement, the re-opening of the Nicholls' murder and more energy being put behind the Bonaty line of inquiry. Inspector Flynn will have to consider this now. Mark my words. We shall push this tonight when we see them.'

20

Flynn household, Greenwich village, New York: 27th January 1922

Inspector Flynn stared out the window, in a sullen silence, like a schoolboy who had been sent to his room for misbehaviour. Bobbie came over and gave him a hug that, although he would not admit it, always helped.

'I'd love to know why, all of a sudden, some members of the public have started raising a hue and cry over the lack of progress on the Rankin case? Nearly forty years on the force and I can count on the fingers of one hand when that has happened.'

'Maybe fellow musicians?' suggested Bobbie, moving out of the way of Mrs Garcia who was moving back and forth between kitchen and dining table like a sentry on picket duty. She growled at Bobbie whenever she went near the dining table.

'Remember to mention you play golf,' said Bobbie.

Flynn looked up at her with an amused frown.

'Have I mentioned that before?' asked Bobbie.

'You might have,' said Flynn patiently. It was probably the tenth time she'd said this in the space of an hour. 'Anyway, how do I look?'

Flynn was wearing the dinner suit he'd last worn on New Year's Eve when he had first met the two English ladies at a party, which ended in murder. He had met them twice since then when they came to the police station to give statements, but had not done so socially, unlike Bobbie.

In a strange way, he was looking forward to seeing the two ladies. Mary was attractive, smart and funny; just the sort of friend he wanted for Bobbie. The old war elephant, Agatha, was quite the most unique woman he'd ever met. A ferocious intelligence and even fiercer tongue. He'd grown to like her immensely and her brother Alastair.

At seven thirty on the dot, they heard the buzzer. The guests had arrived.

'Prompt,' said Flynn, consulting his antique pocket watch. It was five minutes fast and his comment earned an affectionate grin from his daughter who knew about its unreliable timekeeping. Why did men hold onto these old curios when they no longer functioned as they should.

Mrs Garcia went downstairs to the front door and, moments later, they heard voices. Their footsteps echoed up the stairs and then the door opened. Flynn rose to his feet immediately and went over to Agatha, taking both her hands and smiling a welcome. Bobbie and Mary hugged as if they had not seen one another in days, rather than a few hours.

'I'm sorry it's taken you so long to come and visit,' said Flynn, 'And now you'll be leaving soon.'

'Yes, next Friday. Back to Europe,' said Mary. She was missing England now, although her stay in the United States had been eventful.

Mrs Garcia led them to the dining table, where Agatha and Flynn exchanged glances and a wry smile.

'Sorry Lady Frost, no alcohol I'm afraid.'

'Well, it's probably good to give my liver a rest,' replied Agatha wryly.

'I'm not sure I want to hear this' said the policeman drily.

The conversation continued in a similar vein with some light jousting between the Americans, or the 'Colonials' as Agatha referred to them, and the Redcoats. Throughout, Mrs Garcia kept supplying her speciality Mexican dishes which went down very well with the guests. Throughout this period, any mention of current cases was avoided, although Flynn suspected the two ladies were deeply curious. Finally, it was Bobbie who could bear no more of the dancing around the subject.

'I hope you ladies have managed to avoid becoming entangled in any more murder cases,' said Bobbie.

'I hope you have too, young lady. Your father seems rather against you taking an interest if I remember correctly.'

'You do,' murmured Flynn, lighting a cigar.

'How are things going with the murder of that musician? I think I saw Detective Nolan's name mentioned in connection with this case.'

'Not so well,' acknowledged Flynn, puffing on his cigar. 'Not so well at all.'

'Why is that?' asked Agatha, with all due innocence.

Flynn flicked his eyes towards her and there seemed to be some amusement if Bobbie read him correctly. Why indeed, thought Flynn? He had spent most of the afternoon reading the case notes after being hauled into the Commissioner to explain the lack of progress. The next day he fully intended going over to Midtown North precinct to take personal control of the case. He puffed on his cigar a little longer, to give him time to formulate an answer. He was caught between providing the bare bones and missing out on the undoubted intellects of the women or giving more detail and then opening Pandora's Box. Agatha sensing his disquiet, applied the *coup de grace*.

'Yes, I suppose the opinions of a few women in this will smack more of fiction than the sordid world of murder.'

Flynn had the good grace to smile at this and replied, 'I have no doubt that you and my daughter have acquainted yourselves with the details of the case anyway.'

'We have,' acknowledged Agatha.

Flynn's eyes flicked towards two boxes sitting on a desk by the window.

'Those are the case files that have been sent to us from Midtown North. I've been reading through them this afternoon, at the behest of the Commissioner, who is displeased at the lack of progress.'

'I'm sorry to hear that,' said Agatha. 'And that progress is slow. Why do you think that is?'

Flynn shrugged and replied, 'Every so often you come across cases like these. They just have no lead that takes you to the killer. My men have done everything by the book and I can see nothing that would suggest they have missed something in their inquiries.'

Bobbie looked at her father and wondered if he was on the brink of a most unusual admission.

He needed help.

Their help.

Silence fell on the room as Flynn puffed away contentedly on his cigar while the ladies drank tea. It was just after nine thirty in the evening. Outside, New York offered up the sound of horns and sirens by way of accompaniment to the apparent stalemate.

'You are aware of your daughter's theory about Mr Bonaty?'

'I am. And before you decide to lobby for more work to be done on it, I can tell you, Detective Nolan and Yeats have followed this up. They spoke with a Mr Moss today; he sends his regards by the way. I hope you enjoyed the show.'

This was said with no rancour, but Flynn did fix his eyes on his daughter at this point causing her to colour a red almost as deep as her hair.

'They also spoke to Sol Maxim. I gather you met him as well. Another dead end.'

More silence at this revelation. Then Agatha decided to move onto the attack. She glanced over to Mary who removed a sheaf of paper from her handbag.

'You may not have heard, but we have more information on the men that Mr Rankin served with during the War. We saw the photograph.'

This made Flynn sit up and remove the cigar from his mouth.

'How on earth?'

'We paid a visit to Detective Nolan earlier and pooled our information,' said Agatha. She and Mary then proceeded to take Flynn through the information that had come from Chubby. Flynn took some notes and, before he realised it, the dinner party had turned into a meeting to discuss the case. Somewhere deep inside, Flynn had always suspected it would be so.

'None of this proves anything,' pointed out Flynn after he had heard all that Agatha and Mary had said.

'No daddy, but it must give us some cause to re-open the Matt Nicholls' death and look at that once more,' said Bobbie. 'You could get hold of the case file easily. It's Saturday tomorrow. No one would ask questions.'

'What am I looking for?' asked Flynn.

'We need to speak to people who knew Mr Nicholls. Perhaps someone heard him mention Bonaty. I'm convinced this is the key to the whole case,' said Bobbie.

'I'd gathered that, Bobbie,' said Flynn, but not unkindly. Perhaps there was some hope thought Bobbie.

'Let's face it dad. There are no other leads.'

'I'd gathered that too, honey,' murmured Flynn sadly.

This seemed to deflate any optimism in the room. Agatha, sensing that the evening could very soon come to an end, decided to roll the dice.

'Might I propose we go with this theory that Mr Bonaty is somehow involved. Might I also suggest we draw a line between Rankin, Bonaty and Nicholls and the events of that awful day during the War, when their three comrades died who were in the photograph?' suggested Agatha.

'Go on,' said Flynn.

'The next thing I would suggest is that the murderer was known to the victim. You know better than I, Inspector, that this is invariably the case,' continued Agatha.

Flynn nodded.

'That being so, perhaps we should list out those who knew Mr Rankin and speculate on possible motives of which one should be related to the mysterious Mr Bonaty.'

'Where do we start?' asked Mary.

'How about with those who were at the tenement building that morning?' asked Bobbie.

Flynn answered this, 'That was Laszlo, the superintendent. He says he saw no one enter the building except the three tradespeople, all of whom he'd hired and was expecting: Al Eklund, an electrician, Miss Lucy Deng, the cleaner and Glen Fisher, who was there to fix the pipes. The cleaner comes Sunday, Tuesday and Friday. The other two men were called the night before to deal with problems that had sprung up. I think they all seem unlikely suspects to me,' said Flynn.

'Yes,' agreed Agatha. 'Who else?'

'Mr Jones at Feist's Music Publishers?' suggested Bobbie. 'He's connected to Mr Bonaty and Mr Rankin, he served during the War...'

'In a different regiment,' pointed out Flynn, he would have been many miles from Rankin and Nicholls. He was not wounded during the War, so he would not have seen them in a hospital.'

Bobbie's face fell at this. She had him as the number one suspect given his pivotal role across the different players.

'Sol Maxim?' suggested Mary. 'He was the song plugger for Bonaty.'

'He was hired by Ben Strauss,' replied Flynn, who had obviously been studying the case files in great depth. 'Maxim was one of several song pluggers that Strauss has worked with. And Maxim was not in the War. Oh, and final point, he has an alibi for that night and morning. A young lady named Freida.'

'What about Mr Strauss? He's the point of contact with Bonaty. Is he telling the truth?'

Flynn shook his head at this, 'He also has an alibi. He was playing golf at eight. To arrive at the golf course on Long Island from Rankin's apartment would have been a big challenge to say the least. Also, and this is my problem with this Bonaty theory, why would anyone we know be covering up? None of them is Bonaty, he has to be someone else.'

'I agree,' said Agatha quietly.

'Who then?' asked Flynn, a little exasperated. He accepted that it was a loose thread in the investigation, but as far as he could see, it led nowhere.

'Bonaty obviously does not want his identity known,' agreed Agatha. 'There are a lot of reasons why this may be.'

'He's a criminal on the run,' suggested Mary. She did not sound like she believed it.

'Or an established song writer. A bit like a *non de plume*,' added Agatha.

'Why?' interjected Flynn.

'Tax avoidance,' snapped Agatha back. This made Flynn smile and he nodded to the English lady.

'Perhaps the songs aren't his,' said Bobbie. Agatha nodded at this. 'Maybe he stole them from one of the men that died that day.'

Silence greeted this. It was the type of silence you get when everyone has heard a very good idea.

'And Nicholls and Rankin knew this,' said Mary.

'Nicholls knew it first,' said Agatha. 'That's why he was killed. He told Mr Rankin and the killer found out. That may mean blackmail or perhaps they were angry at this Bonaty.'

Flynn was listening intently to this. He knew that his daughter had come up with a new line of inquiry. His feelings about this were mixed of course. He could not avoid feeling fatherly pride that Bobbie had such a sharp mind that she could cut through the confusion to reach a point that felt as if it could be a platform for building a case. Yet he still hated the thought of her in this world.

'It could be anybody then,' said Flynn at last.

'True,' said Mary, 'but the fact remains, you are still potentially looking in the wrong place.'

'Yes, Mary's right,' said Bobbie. 'We need to be looking at the people who knew Matt Nicholls not George Rankin.'

Flynn nodded slowly at this. It made sense. If this hypothesis was correct and, at that moment, it was the only one they had, then they were looking in the wrong place. The killer knew Matt Nicholls first.

'I'll get hold of the Nicholls case file and get someone to work on it,' said Flynn. He ignored the look of satisfaction on his daughter's face. Instead, he thought about how he should go about conducting this line of inquiry. He wanted to be on it personally if only to keep an eye on his daughter. He would need help. It would have to be someone connected with the case that he could trust. That someone would be the person who Flynn had heard was now sidelined in the investigation: Detective Nolan.

21

Flynn household, New York: 29th January 1922

The weekend arrived, which saw Bobbie's time taken up with seeing Violet once more. On Saturday, Bobbie and her father took her to visit Lydia Monk, her great friend before the kidnapping had seen Violet's life overturned. The Monk family were happy to meet up with the Flynns as they felt a debt of gratitude towards them, on a number of levels, not the least of which was the capture of their crooked lawyer.

An energetic game of softball, at least for Bobbie and Violet, took place in Central park where both acquitted themselves well. Bobbie had played softball all her life. Victory had been denied them when Bobbie slipped and twisted her ankle on her final home run.

Sunday saw Flynn enjoying a day's golf with Mary's husband, Kit and his uncle, Alastair, while Bobbie spent another day with Violet. The morning was spent learning how to bake a cake with the help of Mrs Garcia. It was safe to say that Violet made more progress than Bobbie who showed as much facility in the kitchen as her mother had shown, which is to say, none. This fact was pointed out by the housekeeper, in a way that was both complimentary and cruelly funny.

The two cakes sat side by side. One looked as if it had been stood on by a construction worker following an argument over how many eggs had been used. The other was a popular Mexican treat, a three-layer Milk Cake. It stood proudly alongside Bobbie's disastrous effort. Mrs Garcia and Violet stared at Bobbie's creation; heads tilted slightly.

'I'm sure it tastes nice,' said Violet doubtfully.

'You're just like your mother, Red. Beautiful, and useless in the kitchen. Luckily, men have no brains. They'll forgive one if you're good in the other.'

This was cold comfort for Bobbie, who genuinely thought she'd cracked it this time. She burst out laughing and shrugged her shoulders.

'Rather a pessimistic view of men,' suggested Bobbie.

'You'll learn,' said Mrs Garcia enigmatically.

Violet was now fully apprised of the case and wanted to play a part. This, of course, meant the shoe was now on the other foot for Bobbie. As the responsible 'parent', she was keen to protect her ward from any hint of threat. However, Violet had been insistent. As any parent will testify, arguing with a precocious eleven-year-old, who is convinced she is right, can present a potentially insurmountable challenge.

A safe compromise suggested itself to Bobbie and she was rather pleased with the inspiration as it meant that she could kill two birds with one stone: further her knowledge of the area she was investigating as well as taking the first tentative steps towards encouraging Violet to take up music, specifically learn the piano. Bobbie arranged to meet two people she had first met on New Year's Eve. They were two members of a band called The Troopers.

Albrecht 'Fritz' Keeler and Tommy 'the Trump' Jackson were two members of a band called The Troopers. Both were musicians as well as songwriters who were one day hoping to break into the lucrative music publishing business, like dozens of other hopefuls in New York.

Fritz managed The Troopers and had doubled their number of engagements since taking up the role almost a year earlier by the simple expediency of having them turn up on time and not high. He was German and had fought in the War. This fact had not prevented the United States accepting him as they had accepted the tired and the poor huddled masses yearning to breathe free.

The two men were delighted to meet Bobbie again and meet Violet. The first thing they had noticed was Bobbie's heavily strapped ankle and her wooden cane. A little name calling ensued as Tommy referred to Bobbie as Charlie, after Charlie Chaplin, whose cane resembled the one Bobbie was using.

After a few minutes telling them about their softball in the park, and Bobbie's accident, conversation turned to the case and the show, "*Heaven's Below*". The two men had seen the show which helped. Bobbie was careful not to reveal too much of what she knew. She was interested in what the two men thought of the show.

'I liked the show. The songs were good. I don't know who Bonaty is but he knows what he's doing.'

'I want to see the show,' said Violet.

Bobbie frowned at this as did the two men. It was somewhat risqué in parts and Violet, despite having an old head on her shoulders, was too young.

'Let's give it a year or two,' suggested Bobbie.

To help Bobbie change the subject away from the show, Tommy asked Violet, 'You got a young man, Miss Violet?'

By way of revenge for Bobbie not allowing her to see the show, Violet revealed one aspect of the case that was bound to put Bobbie in the spotlight.

'I don't need one of those,' opined the young girl, but then, turning to Bobbie and smiling, she added, 'Bobbie has a sweetheart though.'

This shocked Bobbie, 'I do not. Don't listen to her.'

'Who?' asked Tommy, ignoring Bobbie's frantic frown.

'A detective called Nolan,' announced Violet, with a grin. She folded her arms and sat back to enjoy Bobbie's embarrassment.

Nolan had been one of the investigating officers on New Year's Eve when Bobbie had met the Troopers.

'He's a good-looking guy,' acknowledged Tommy.

'A dreamboat,' corrected Violet.

'Who's not my boyfriend,' interjected Bobbie, smiling despite herself.

'As the young lady says,' replied Tommy, also smiling, 'You don't need one of those anyhow.'

Violet was not one to exhaust a subject. She'd stirred up a nice mess of mortification for Bobbie, it was time to move on. They were sitting by a piano, so it seemed natural to her to find out more about what they did as musicians.

'How do you write a song?' asked Violet, fascinated and enchanted by the two men.

'Usually we start with the music,' said Fritz. 'Every song these days follows the same pattern.'

'Really?' asked Bobbie. 'I hadn't realised.'

'Oh yes,' said Tommy. 'Everything is thirty-two bars, broken up by four eight bar units. The structure is AABA. So, you have the same melody repeated three times with one variation in the middle.'

'Seems a little limiting,' observed Bobbie.

'It can be, but you get used to it,' replied Tommy.

'So, what does that mean in a song?' asked Violet.

Fritz played a part of a melody from one of the hit songs from "*Heaven's Below*", a love song called "*Right Girl, Wrong Time*" while Tommy began to sing.

I found romance, it felt divine,
A girl so pure and forever,
to think as mine.
Now someone's led her

Tommy broke off from singing and addressed Violet, 'That's the first A. It leads onto the second.' He began to sing again.

Astray, away, I felt so bad.
She was my girl, but no longer.
Now, It's all so sad,
'Cause I never wronged her.

Tommy's smooth crooning danced lightly over the words yet managed to convey the melancholy of the song. Violet listened enraptured. When Tommy had finished, she gave Bobbie a sour look and said, 'I think you're mean not to let me see the show.'

'When you're older,' said Bobbie, Tommy and Fritz in unison. This was enough to make Violet chuckle and she gave up bombarding Bobbie on the subject.

They parted half an hour later, with the boys inviting Bobbie and Violet to see them play, with further guidance on the redundancy of men generally, and boyfriends in particular. There was no argument from either lady, although at least one of them harboured doubts about the advice.

Bobbie and Violet returned to the orphanage. Each time they parted; Bobbie could sense the regret in Violet. She felt it herself. She missed Violet during the week and wondered if she was ready yet to consider coming to live with them. Violet was wondering the same, yet as much as she wanted to raise the subject, she wouldn't. The fear of rejection was overwhelming. She was desperate for Bobbie to raise the topic also. It hung in the air between them as they parted.

Sister Assumpta took Violet's hand and led her back inside the old building; she sensed Violet was close to tears so she didn't look at her. Instead, she allowed Violet to have her moment of sadness in private. They walked together along the long corridor. The only sounds were of their footsteps echoing on the parquet floor and of children screaming outside.

They went into the dining room where some sandwiches awaited the young girl. Sister Assumpta sat with her as she ate. Still, they did not speak. Violet was happy to feel the old nun's loving gaze upon her. It was a comfort. When Violet had finished, Sister Assumpta took her hand.

'Tell me, my child, if that young lady were to ask you to come and live with her and her father, would you?'

The tears that welled up in Violet's eyes were the only answer to such a question. The nun smiled at Violet and leaned forward to kiss her on the forehead.

Just then the door that led to the playground burst open and the noise of the children outside grew louder.

A young girl shouted inside, 'Hey Violet, are you coming outside?'

Sister Assumpta nodded towards the door and said, 'Off you go. It'll be bedtime soon.'

22

Tribune Building, New York: 30th January 1922

Monday rolled around again, as it usually does, with all the gleeful bonhomie of a hangover. Bobbie limped off to the Tribune Building twirling her cane while her father went to follow up on the death of Matt Nicholls. His first stop, however, was to pick up Detective Nolan, before heading north of Manhattan to the 4th precinct in Yonkers, to collect the case files on the Nicholls' suicide.

Bobbie usually arrived early at the office on a Monday, to catch up on the deaths of the great and the good over the weekend. Buckner Fanning was there when she arrived. This was the first time in a while that he had been in the office before her on a Monday. Normally, he would grunt a good morning before settling down to work and leaving Bobbie to get on with what she had to do. This morning was different. He called her over to his desk.

Looking over his rimless spectacles at Bobbie, he addressed her in a manner that seemed slightly different from his semi-sneer. It was almost as if he felt uncomfortable. Like he was about to break bad news. In some senses he was.

'Miss Flynn,' he said, before pausing and looking down at a piece of paper that probably contained an obituary to be updated. 'I don't know if you are aware of a death that happened on Friday.'

Bobbie shook her head, but she felt a chill descend on her because Fanley's manner seemed so ill at ease.

'It's up to you, I can do this if you would prefer,' he said, glancing towards the piece of paper.

'Who is it?' asked Bobbie, curious.

'Elizabeth Cochran passed away,' said Fanley, pausing for a moment. Then he was about to add something when Bobbie interrupted him.

'Nellie Bly,' said Bobbie, unable to stop her eyes filling with tears. She reached out to take the obituary. 'I'd like to, if I may.'

Fanley nodded and handed her the piece of paper. He said, 'That is quite an old one. A little short. It needs more.' He stopped speaking for a moment, as if trying to find the right words to brief Bobbie adequately on telling the story of a legendary female journalist. She had made her name working undercover, as an inmate of an asylum, to reveal the deplorable conditions experienced by women in these institutions. Then he added, 'I think we will need to devote half a page at least. Can you see to it?'

'Yes, Mr Fanley,' whispered Bobbie. She turned and went back to her seat. Thankfully, she was able to sit with her back to Fanley, as it allowed her tears to fall freely for the woman who had inspired her to become a journalist; the woman who had created the idea of investigative journalism.

Bobbie's morning was split between writing up the remarkable story and shedding yet more tears as she recalled the remarkable life. Mercifully, Fanley left her alone to finish the piece which she handed to him a little after midday. He took it from her and noted that she had written three pages on the life of the dead journalist, who had used the name Nellie Bly for her columns.

Fanley glanced at it then nodded to Bobbie. While it wasn't a standing ovation by any means it meant a lot to Bobbie that she had been allowed to devote so much time and so many words to someone that to her was a hero.

Bobbie sat down at her typewriter; her fingers floated over the keys, then they pounced, pounding away, crafting the tribute this woman deserved.

```
Goodbye Nellie Bly. We never met but
you were my hero. You showed me what I
and other women could be. This is meant
to be an obituary but I can only write a
eulogy dedicated to your life, your
achievements, your inspiration, for your
life deserves nothing less.
```

Around one in the afternoon, Bobbie met Agatha and Mary for lunch at Harper's, a restaurant often frequented by journalists from the Tribune building. Bobbie spied Damon Runyan there, lunching with her editor Thornton Kent. He was one of the few journalists that was ever allowed to do this. Bobbie pointed the two men out as they ordered their food.

After the first few minutes while Bobbie explained the reason for her limp and the use of a cane, Agatha moved on to business.

'So, your father is now on the case?' she asked, her eyes sparkling with curiosity.

'Yes,' confirmed Bobbie. 'He went to Yonkers to follow up on the alleged suicide of Matt Nicholls.'

'It was murder,' said Mary.

There was going to be no argument, from her dinner companions, on this score. Sadly, there seemed little that they could do until the case files came back and her father had begun to meet people connected with the dead musician.

'Is anyone helping him?' asked Mary, just as their lunch arrived.

Bobbie paused a moment which caused her two companions to glance up from their lunch.

'Does your silence mean that he is working with Detective Nolan?' asked Agatha, getting directly to the point.

Bobbie rolled her eyes but decided not to respond to the gentle ribbing, implied if not in the question, then in the raised eyebrows and half-smile from the questioner.

'At least all is forgiven,' said Mary brightly. Before adding mischievously, 'Another opportunity to go undercover with the delectable Detective Nolan.'

Bobbie erupted into laughter at this. There was little point in being defensive anyway. It would only be an open invitation to the two Englishwomen to keep the vaguely ribald allusions coming.

Towards the end of their meal, a gangly individual approached the table. He was wearing a tweed jacket, which was a little too small for him and round spectacles with a little tape on the corner.

'Hey Bobbie, how are you?' said Toby Marner or "Two-Brained" Toby as he was known in the newspaper offices.

'Hello Toby,' said Bobbie, smiling up at her colleague. Introductions were made between Toby and the two Englishwomen.

'I think I saw you all last week.'

'Really? Where?'

'I decided to take in that show, "*Heaven's Below*" and I was looking around the crowd and saw you in a box near the front of the stage. I tried waving but you didn't see me.'

'What did you think of the show?'

Toby's face fell a little and he replied, 'Not my taste, I'm afraid. I was curious because of the writer, you know, the one you said was this great enigma.'

'O. Bonaty,' said Bobbie.

'That's the one,' replied Toby. He shook his head, and was about to wander off, when a thought seemed to strike him. He said, 'It's strange no one's mentioned it before now.'

'Mentioned what?' asked Bobbie.

'The name.'

Over the years, Agatha's patience levels had gone in the opposite direction to her age. And she'd never been very patient to begin with. Watching Toby talk around what he was meant to be talking about was beginning to wear by now. If there is a point to be made then, in her view, you should make it or move on. Toby seemed to be one of that breed of man that beats around the bush and then forgets what was in the bush to begin with. Her finger began tapping ominously on the table. Mary noted the storm a-gathering and decoded the situation to nudge their visitor towards his point.

'Is there something wrong about the name?' suggested Mary with eyebrows raised in a questioning manner.

'Well, yes. It's an anagram,' replied the crossword creator of the *New York American*.

This announcement was greeted with stunned silence at the table. Agatha was the first to react to the news. She turned to a waitress who was passing just at that moment and pointed to her pen. The waitress handed it over to Agatha, who quickly wrote something on the white napkin in front of her. She held it up to "Two-Brained" Toby who smiled and nodded in approval.

'If you ever fancy working with me in crosswords you are very welcome,' said the newspaper's resident crossword creator.

An hour later, Chubby Chadderton arrived at his offices in Whitehall in London. He smiled at Miss Brooks and, as the office was empty except for them both, wondered if he might get away with a kiss. Such foolish romantic notions were swiftly abandoned with Miss Brooks' first words.

'There's a telegram from Lady Frost on your desk.'

'Oh,' said Chubby straightening up. 'Better see what she wants, I suppose.'

He opened the door to his office that was a veritable jungle of paper, much to Miss Brooks' despair. He found the envelope on the desk. He ripped it open and swiftly read the instructions, for it was always an instruction, when it came to Agatha.

'Oh,' he said once more before putting his head through the door and looking out into the outer office. 'Have you seen...?'

'Yes. Lady Frost wants us to investigate who was working at the hospital at Bouleuse on 15th July 1918,' said Miss Brooks. She was the very epitome of an organised secretary.

'We should get John...'

'I already have,' smiled Miss Brooks. Chubby looked at Miss Brooks. Miss Brooks looked at Chubby. The office was officially empty except for them. The romantic possibilities were all too apparent and despite the fact they had only parted company an hour previously, Chubby prevailed upon Miss Brooks, without too much apparent demurral from the young lady in question, for a kiss or three.

23

It was early evening at the Jackson Theatre. There were some theatregoers beginning to arrive for the performance later. Many were there to queue up for returns while others just wanted to take in the atmosphere of a rare trip into Broadway. Late January and the days were getting a little longer, but certainly not much warmer.

Bobbie hobbled her way through the Broadway crowds to the stage door. A man at the door blocked her entrance. He stared at her and wondered if she was a dancer in the show. She certainly had the looks.

'I've come to see Sol Maxim,' explained Bobbie.

'Name?' asked the man, reaching for a clipboard with a sheet of paper on it.

Bobbie gave her name and prayed that the musician had remembered to mention it at the stage door.

He had.

Bobbie passed through and headed towards the orchestra pit where they had arranged to meet. The area backstage was as crowded and as loud as the Broadway itself. Bobbie noted that it was mostly young women. The show, she remembered, had been rather reliant on underclad young women performing various song and dance routines. She suspected that this had contributed enormously to its popularity.

She wasn't sure how she felt about this. On the one hand, it contributed to a rather narrow prejudice about women generally and about performers specifically. Yet, there was no question that the sounds she was hearing, delighted laughter and the excitement all around her and in the dressing rooms were intoxicating and she could hardly begrudge these girls their moment in the sun.

How many of them had enjoyed a private education as she had? This was their way to make a living, to be a little independent. There was not going to be any resolution to the conflict she felt, so she swept it from her mind and focused on finding Maxim.

She remembered from their backstage tour a few days earlier, the route to the orchestra pit and negotiated it without getting lost. She was also helped by the sound of a few of the musicians playing some discordant notes.

The door leading to the orchestra pit was opened and she spotted Maxim in his usual spot. The arrival of a beautiful redhead in a very male-oriented orchestra was always going to raise heads, including Maxim's. He smiled and waved to her. The other musicians looked on enviously as Bobbie waved at him and made her way over. Sol Maxim was going to enjoy the envy of the others for all he was worth.

When Bobbie arrived, he gave her a hug and treated her like she was just one of many girlfriends he could call upon in his life. As Bobbie had come for an important piece of evidence, she was happy to play along, especially as he gave her a cheeky wink before he'd hugged her. Men could be such children, she'd long since decided.

'What happened to you?' asked Maxim pointing to Bobbie's cane and the strapping on her ankle.

'I was on a home run and then I wasn't,' laughed Bobbie.

They chatted about the case for a short while as the little musician was curious about how things were going.

'I do have a few more questions, Mr Maxim,' said Bobbie. The two of them were sharing the piano stool and Bobbie was very much aware that almost everyone was pretending not to look at them. Maxim was delighted to extend his time with Bobbie, so was more than willing to answer extra questions.

'Did you ever hear the name Matt Nicholls?' asked Bobbie.

Maxim thought for a minute and then shook his head. He said, 'Sorry, Miss Flynn, the name doesn't mean anything to me.'

'I don't suppose Mr Strauss ever mentioned if anyone ever accused Bonaty of plagiarism or stealing the songs?'

This brought a laugh from Maxim. He looked at Bobbie as if she were a guileless young child and said, 'Miss Flynn, this happens all the time. As soon as someone has a hit song, someone comes out of the woodwork and claims they wrote it first. They'll change the name and put some different words, pretend it's theirs. They try and shake down publishers with threats of lawsuits. No one pays much attention to these things now. I don't know if this happened with Mr Bonaty, but I've no reason to think it wouldn't.'

'You think I should speak with Mr Strauss?' asked Bobbie.

'I would. I'm sure he might have kept the names of the accusers on file. You never know I suppose,' said Maxim. 'I'd speak with Feist's as well. They're more likely to have kept the names.'

'Thanks, that's a good idea. I shall. Anyway, were you able to bring the sheet music?'

Sol Maxim's smile was a little forced, but being the trouper he was he maintained it as he handed over a few pages of sheet music to Bobbie.

'Look after that Miss Flynn,' he said.

'I shall. And I shall return it to you soon. We need to make a copy of it, but when we do, I'll bring it back to you.'

She rose from her seat and gave Maxim a long, sisterly hug and winked to the musician. The smile this provoked from him made her feel that he had earned something more so she pecked him on the cheek. This almost brought an audible groan from the other young men in the pit, but Maxim was too happy to care.

Around six in the evening, Bobbie was in a cab with Agatha and Mary heading to the offices of Ben Strauss. It was a risk insofar as he may have left for the day, but Agatha insisted that they take the chance. She then spent the whole journey urging the cab driver to "step on it", which he gladly obliged as there was a five-dollar bonus in it for him.

They screeched to a halt outside the offices of the lawyer and were relieved to see that the lights were on. The cab driver went away with his well-earned tip while the ladies crossed over the road to try and gain a few precious minutes with Strauss.

They knocked on the door and waited to see if someone would open it. There was no reply. Agatha used the handle of her umbrella to give the brass plate of Ben Strauss & Co a rather more robust knock. Bobbie and Mary both cringed slightly as it seemed she might take the door off its hinges.

It worked.

A minute later the door was opened by, a rather surprised, Ben Strauss.

'Ladies, you're back,' he said. He did not seem unwelcoming or put out at Agatha's rather insistent knocking.

'Mr Strauss,' said Agatha. 'Would you mind sparing us just a couple of minutes of your valuable time? We shan't detain you long, we promise.'

The prospect of another few minutes with Bobbie and Mary was perhaps not the worst offer that Strauss would ever receive and he happily consented.

'I have plenty of time, ladies, please come in.'

They followed Strauss to his office and sat down, once more, on the sofa.

'We are still following up on the mysterious Bonaty,' said Bobbie. 'We were wondering if many people had ever come forward with accusations of plagiarism.'

Strauss laughed out loud at this and seemed genuinely amused by the question.

'Miss Flynn, this happens all the time,' said Strauss, in the manner of a parent to a child.

'How did you deal with those accusations?' asked Bobbie.

Strauss shrugged and said, 'We mostly ignore them. If they came from song writers coming to the office threatening to sue us, we would throw them out on their ear. If it came from another lawyer, we would pass the details onto Leo Feist or whichever publisher we were dealing with. There would always be a denial of any wrongdoing on our part.'

'So, Mr Feist has the details of these accusations?' continued Bobbie.

'Only the ones where the complainant had a lawyer acting for them. And then the complainant would have to get their case heard. Only then would we be called upon to act on Mr Bonaty's behalf. Otherwise, both Feist and Bonaty would end up paying thousands to defend themselves against these people.'

'How many tried their luck?' asked Mary.

Strauss thought for a second and said, 'Well, I seem to remember there were maybe half a dozen or more, but only a couple of them went through a lawyer. Feist will have the details, I'm sure. Nothing ever came of them; I do know that. Once these people see that it might take months or years to have their case heard and they see how much money it will cost them, then they give up. They think it's going to be easy money to shakedown a music publisher. It's not, trust me. Feist has been in this game a long time. He knows what he's doing. You just can't come off the streets and shake down a man like that.'

'Do you think you have any letters in your Bonaty files relating to plagiarism?'

Strauss was unsure. He pointed to the bank of large filing cabinets.

'Let me take a look.'

A few moments later he extracted a file relating to the songwriter. He set it down on his desk and quickly leafed through any correspondence there. Finally, he looked up and said, 'I'm sorry, there's nothing here. I guess any threatening letters were thrown away. As I said, if the letter had come from Feist or from a lawyer, we would have kept it as this would have meant things were a little more serious. Your best bet is Mr Feist.'

'Mr Strauss,' asked Bobbie. 'Does the name Matt Nicholls ring a bell?'

Strauss thought for a moment then replied, 'I do remember one guy coming to the office. I didn't like the look of him. I threw him out myself. I think he said his name was Nicholls.'

The ladies thanked him for his time before leaving. It wasn't much, but at least they could connect Nicholls with the lawyer. However, the lack of any letters was a problem. They needed evidence. Agatha tried to put a brave face on their disappointment.

'It's only a tactical setback, not the end of the war.'

'True,' agreed Mary. 'We'll call on Mr Feist tomorrow morning and see if he has anything that can help us. It sounds as if he's the more likely source. Perhaps Chubby will have come up trumps by then.'

Bobbie's face fell slightly. The two ladies noticed this.

'Would you mind if we made it late morning. There's somewhere I have to be. Unless you both wanted to join me.'

When Agatha and Mary heard the reason for delaying going to the music publisher, they immediately assented.

24

Later that evening, around eleven o'clock, Bobbie could be found, in a neat reversal of roles, pacing back and forward in her living room, like a father waiting for his daughter to return home from a date. This was typical for her father to be late returning home, when working on a case. Since his promotion upstairs as an inspector, these occasions were far fewer. This had the paradoxical impact of giving Flynn back more time in his life while making him a little less happy. He liked nothing more than the hunt. Now he was one or two steps removed from having a direct impact on cases these days, except on rare occasions.

This, thanks to Agatha's unusual intervention, was now one of those occasions.

Bobbie heard a key in the door downstairs just after eleven and then the thump of Flynn's footsteps coming up the stairs. He walked into the living room and was surprised to see his daughter waiting for him wearing flame red pyjamas.

'What time do you call this?' said Bobbie in a stern voice before adding, mischievously, 'Have you been out with that young detective again, Nolan?'

Despite himself, Flynn laughed and shook his head. It was a further sign that the frost in their relationship, over Bobbie's involvement in the case and with Detective Nolan, had now thawed sufficiently for Flynn to see the humour in the situation.

'I wish I could have a drink,' he said.

'Why don't you?' replied Bobbie.

The answer was that he had sworn to uphold the Volstead Act, despite its manifest stupidity. This did not need to be said, so he remained silent. His mackintosh came off and was thrown towards the sofa. It missed. This prompted a few 'Tsks' from Bobbie, which sounded so much like Nancy, his wife, that Flynn was forced to glance away from his daughter. Bobbie picked the coat up and went to hang it up on the wooden coat stand. Flynn threw his hat in the direction of the stand and it was expertly caught by Bobbie who added it to the other hats, all hers, already on the stand.

'How was your day?' asked Bobbie. In many other households such a question might have been seen as just a polite way of showing interest, in something that was of no consequence to the listener. This was not the case just at that moment. Bobbie was intensely curious about how her father's day had gone.

Flynn sighed and did not so much sit as fall onto the sofa. He looked all in and Bobbie felt a stab of guilt for asking him to rifle through his memory of the day, sort out the wheat from the proverbial chaff and then talk through what had happened all while he desperately craved bed.

'Maybe I'm too old for this,' he began.

'Nonsense,' said Bobbie, with feeling. She sat beside him and added, 'Are you sure I can't find something for you?'

'Honestly, a tea would be fine.'

A few minutes later Bobbie returned with a tea and saw her father with his feet up on the table reading through his notes from the day.

'You don't have to,' said Bobbie, handing him the cup.

This made Flynn laugh and he ignored her obvious falsehood.

'So, we met with the cops at 4th precinct and got the lowdown on the alleged suicide. They were happy to hand over the case notes. It looks like they have enough on their plate. Nolan and I met with the folk at Nicholls' apartments. Everyone said the same thing, he was a suicide waiting to happen; always drunk. Just a very unhappy man.'

'Friends?'

'This is where it does get interesting. We met some people that he'd played with over the last few months and a couple confirmed what you've been saying, that the Bonaty show has been stolen from someone who died that day at the battle of Marne.'

'Do we know who?'

'No. He never said and we can find nothing, in what's left of his belongings, where he might have written it down.'

'Relatives?'

Flynn shook his head and then sipped some of his tea. After a few moments he continued, 'None in New York and none that seemed to care. No brothers or sisters and his parents died years ago. It sounds like he was pretty lonely.'

'How sad,' said Bobbie. 'So, there are no things left that belong to Mr Nicholls that we can search through?'

'Correct. It's all gone. The guys at the precinct didn't remember seeing anything to do with "*Heaven's Below*", but I'm not sure they really looked.'

Bobbie's face fell a little as she listened. She said, 'I suppose there's not much point if you believe it was a suicide anyway. Was there a suicide note?'

'Yes, but it was pretty short and not so sweet. Something like, *I can't go on. It's better like this.*'

'I see,' said Bobbie. 'Did you find any connection to George Rankin?'

'A few of his bandmates remembered Rankin and they remember Miss Montez.'

'She is very attractive,' added Bobbie.

'That's men for you,' said Flynn, wryly. 'They said Rankin had come to see them play once or twice with Miss Montez and then a couple of times on his own. This coincided with Nicholls becoming more volatile. At first, they blamed Rankin for the change, but that's when they heard him say that the Bonaty show was stolen. They think he wrote to Bonaty's lawyer and then Feist's but never heard anything back. So, he went to see Feist's, directly, but he didn't get to meet anyone. They threw him out.'

'Mr Jones did not mention having seen Mr Nicholls or, even, knowing much about him coming to the office,' mused Bobbie.

'I'm not surprised,' replied Flynn. 'If Nicholls was not allowed into the office, then Jones might not have been told. I'm sure Nicholls was not the first or the last man to try his luck with them.'

'So why didn't Mr Rankin help? He was with Feist?' asked Bobbie. This seemed puzzling to her.

'I can think of one reason,' replied her father. 'He didn't want to cause trouble for himself. The last thing he would have needed was to lose his job as a song plugger. That doesn't mean he didn't try to find out though. In fact, it's possible he did say something after Nicholls was killed or committed suicide, if you believe that, which I don't.'

'It looks like you need to speak to the music publisher, dad, to find out what he knew,' said Bobbie, knowing full well that was exactly what she intended doing with Agatha and Mary.

'I won't have time tomorrow,' said Flynn. 'I have to follow up on a few things with Nicholls and then see the Commissioner on how the case is progressing. I've heard Grimm is driving everyone nuts. They're spending more time writing up what they have done than doing any actual investigating. I could suggest to him that he and Yeats go.'

This was not ideal. Grimm either did not know about the Bonaty angle, or he simply did not care.

Bobbie pointed this out, 'Why would Lieutenant Grimm go to Feist's? You would have to waste time briefing him on the Bonaty angle and I must admit, we don't have any evidence to support the theory. I have a better idea.'

Flynn raised a sceptical eyebrow at this, which suggested he knew what was coming. Bobbie pressed ahead anyway, 'I could go, daddy. I mean, they already know me.'

'Why do I get the feeling you were going to go anyway?' said Flynn, grumpily, before rising to his feet and adding, 'I need my bed.'

25

Woodlawn Cemetery, New York: 31st January 1922

A bitterly cold breeze swept across the graveyard, through the headstones as if the occupants had risen, en masse, to attend the funeral of Elizabeth Cochrane. It was noticeable to Bobbie and her friends, just how many of those in attendance were women. There were hundreds of people in attendance. Bobbie recognised many of them as leading lights of the women's rights movement in New York. All seemed to pull their coats around themselves a little more tightly in a choreographed movement. Bobbie was sure Nellie Bly would have been amused by this.

The coffin was slowly lowered into the ground and Bobbie wept, unashamedly, as did most, to see a heroine of women's rights and a leading light of journalism, laid to rest. Much to Bobbie's surprise, she saw Thornton Kent in attendance, standing alongside other men, always men, who were editors of rival newspapers. Just for one morning, this rivalry was set aside as they paid their respects to one of their own.

One of their own.

When would women be seen, as Nellie Bly had been, not just as a female journalist, but simply as a journalist, wondered Bobbie? As a fellow co-worker. A colleague. Despite the astonishing life the deceased had led, Bobbie felt women were no closer yet to being equal in the eyes of the law. It would take generations before men saw them this way.

One battle at a time.

After the internment, Bobbie and the two ladies walked away to a waiting cab. Bobbie directed the cabbie to take them across town to Leo Feist's office on 28th street. They managed to beat the rush away from the cemetery. On the way over, they discussed how they would handle the interview with either Mr Feist or young Mr Jones.

'It might be better if it is the young man,' said Agatha.

Mary grinned at this and they both looked meaningfully at Bobbie. It was quite clear what meaning lay behind the look, which made Bobbie colour a little but she could not help smiling, despite herself.

Changing the subject, Mary asked Bobbie, 'Did your father say anything about the Nicholls' case?'

'I didn't see him for long last night,' admitted Bobbie. 'When he's on a case he becomes almost obsessed until they find the person they're after. And he was out of the house before I could see him this morning. It doesn't sound as if they have very much.'

'Pity,' said Agatha.

Bobbie was less sure they'd really missed anything, by not seeing him. She said, 'I don't think he would have said much anyway. He can be like a bear with a sore head.'

'Well maybe he'll open up more if we discover something from Mr Feist.'

It took over twenty minutes to drive across the city from the Bronx to 28th street where they dropped Bobbie off at the music publisher.

'Let's hope Mr Feist's record keeping is better than that of Mr Strauss,' said Agatha. 'We'll wait here while you work your charms on Mr Jones.'

Bobbie did not have the same confidence as her friends on this score. She walked into the lobby of the offices where she saw the same woman behind the desk that they had met a few days previously. The woman seemed to recognise Bobbie, which was hardly a surprise, as she was probably more used to young men, clutching a file full of dreams.

'Good morning,' said Bobbie. 'Would it be possible to see Mr Jones for a few moments. I won't detain him very long.'

The woman nodded and called up via the intercom to the upstairs office. Very soon the young woman they had met before, Miss Summer, came down to meet them. While she retained her usual, and very impeccable, professional manner, the sight of the young woman perhaps, brought out a certain territorial instinct. Her manner was at the chilly end of courteous.

Miss Summer led Bobbie upstairs, in silence, before disappearing for a few moments into the office of Mr Jones. She reappeared a minute later, followed by Nick Jones, who looked so happy to see Bobbie again. He still sported the tweed jacket and bow tie and was even smoking a pipe. If his intention had been to add ten years to his appearance then, to Bobbie, he had succeeded magnificently.

'This is a pleasant surprise,' said Jones and nothing, in his smile or bright eyes, suggested this was anything less than the truth. Miss Summer turned her back on him and went to her desk outside the two offices.

'I don't wish to take up any of your valuable time,' said Bobbie. 'But I do have an unusual request.'

The eyes of the young man flitted towards Bobbie and a silent prayer was offered. It would go unanswered.

'It relates to your client, O. Bonaty.'

'I had a feeling it would,' laughed Jones. 'Why don't you come into my office and we'll see how I can help you.'

Bobbie followed Jones into the office. She avoided glancing in the direction of Miss Summer for fear of being burned alive by the molten hatred she sensed coming from the young woman.

Jones was gentleman enough or, at least, intent on impressing enough, to wait for Bobbie to sit down before he did so himself.

'What has Mr Bonaty done now?' asked Jones, with laughter in his voice.

'Have you any records of accusations being levelled against Bonaty of plagiarism?' asked Bobbie quickly. This question was, perhaps, not the one Jones had anticipated and his face fell a little. On a number of levels, it was rather troubling, not the least of which was why a young woman, who was an obituary writer, was wanting to rake up these old accusations. The fact that she was rather beautiful made it all the more disappointing.

Another risk that Bobbie had discussed with her friends on the way over, was that such a question might provoke a certain amount of defensiveness in the music publisher as it could be perceived as a bid by a newspaper to start muckraking in search of some headlines. This was a very sensitive issue and would need to be handled with great care.

Bobbie added quickly, 'The reason for asking is that a man was found dead just before Christmas, Matt Nicholls, who may have made such a claim. I don't suppose the name means anything to you?'

The face of the music publisher seemed to relax, in the face of Bobbie's earnest prettiness. She didn't quite flutter her eyelashes, but the way she fixed her eyes on Jones certainly would have had both Mary and Agatha silently nodding in approval.

'The name doesn't ring a bell,' admitted Jones. 'You know, we get a lot of this and it's usually hogwash.

'I'm sure it is,' agreed Bobbie, nodding with Jones.

Jones pressed the intercom and said, 'Miss Summer, can you bring in the Bonaty file and any file we may have relating to plagiarism lawsuits. Thank you.' Jones smiled at his visitor. He liked smiling. And why not, his teeth were rather becoming in their straightness and whiteness. The smile, however, had a certain forced quality to it. Jones remained outwardly friendly, but there was no missing the hard undercurrent to his next comment.

'I'm sure we can put this to bed very soon. I gather from Strauss that there are some English ladies considering bringing this show to the West End in London.' The second part of the statement was like a warning shot to Bobbie. The warning read: don't mess with this show.

'Oh, that's exciting,' said Bobbie, pretending to be excited for the music publisher.

'Yes, the last thing we need is any hint that there is any question over the provenance of these songs,' said Jones. His face was still smiling, but there was no missing the hint of a threat contained within what he'd said.

Bobbie did not reply to this because just at that moment, Miss Summer came in with two files and set them down on Jones' desk.

'Could you take a look in the plagiarism file, Miss Summer and see if there is any correspondence related to Mr Bonaty?' Jones picked up the file and handed it to Miss Summer. Then he opened the Bonaty file and quickly leafed through the sheaf of papers contained therein.

As he did this his head shook and he muttered repeatedly, 'Nope, nope, no, not that.'

Finally, he reached the end of the file and smiled at Bobbie.

'Nothing here about any lawsuit or claims against him on the grounds of plagiarism,' said Jones. He glanced over at Miss Summer who also shook her head but said nothing.

'I'm pretty sure we've had the usual poison pen letters, but we just throw those away. Anyone can write that kind of nonsense.'

'Then it's only when the letter comes from a lawyer or another publisher?' asked Bobbie.

'Correct,' said Jones, rising to his feet. By doing so he was signalling the end of the meeting. Bobbie took the hint and rose from her seat also. She held out her hand and smiled a thank you.

Jones held onto her hand a fraction longer than good manners would have deemed acceptable and Bobbie gave a silent thanks to Miss Summers whose presence probably had saved her from fending off a potential advance from the young man before her.

'I'm sorry that we could not help you more, Miss Flynn. If you need anything else, please let me know. You know we can get tickets for any show on Broadway if you're ever interested.'

Bobbie was not interested but decided that a smile might ensure the door was not shut firmly to any other help she may need in the case.

A few minutes later, Bobbie was back in the cab and breaking the bad news to Agatha and Mary. Once more, Agatha was surprisingly philosophical about the lack of any progress.

'I suppose it was always likely that they would not want to keep such accusations on file. No matter, I do not see this as a setback.'

Bobbie did and her glum face could not hide the disappointment.

'Patience, child. Don't forget, we still have a few irons in the fire,' said Agatha kindly, seeing the evident disappointment on Bobbie's face.

Once more, a lot was riding on what information could be found in England. Agatha was unwilling to admit this, but it was something of a last chance for their end of the investigation. Bobbie, however, had already worked this out.

'Looks like it's up to your friend, Chubby,' said Bobbie sadly, before resting her chin on her hand and staring out at the lunchtime crowds jostling on the sidewalks of 5th Avenue.

26

Bobbie elected to return with Agatha and Mary to their apartment in the Hotel des Artistes on west 67th Street. Her father was unlikely to be home until late and she preferred the company of her unusual and very entertaining friends. There was also the prospect that news might have come through from England.

It had.

When they reached the apartment that Agatha and her brother, Alastair, were renting, they were greeted by Alastair's housekeeper, Ella-Mae. Bobbie had met Ella-Mae on New Year's Eve, so no introductions were necessary. The diminutive housekeeper handed Agatha a large envelope. The eyes of the three ladies widened in excitement. They immediately walked over to the dining table to examine the contents.

'I must say, your friend has come up with the goods again,' said Bobbie as they took their seats.

'Let's hope so, Bobbie,' said Agatha. 'I think we must face facts. If we cannot find any name in here that connects us to this case then I think we shall have to wait and see how your father's inquiries are progressing. That would be most vexing.'

'I agree,' said Bobbie. More like her father than her father would ever like to admit, she was as obsessive and competitive, about finding the killer as he was. 'Well, let's have a look.'

Mary tore open the envelope which contained a list of names and a few words from Chubby at the top.

LIST OF STAFF WORKING AT H.O.E BOULEUSE DEALING WITH CASUALTIES FROM SECOND BATTLE MARNE FROM 15TH TO 20TH JULY 1918.
CHUBBY

Below this brief introduction was a list of the doctors, nurses and administrative staff who were on duty during the first few terrible days following the last big German offensive at Marne. Mary handed the list over to Bobbie to peruse. Bobbie put her finger on the first name and then slowly and methodically ran it down over each name.

For some reason Bobbie was holding her breath as she studied each name. When she reached the second page she finally exhaled, but still no name looked familiar.

Then, halfway down the final page she stopped.

'Oh my,' she said and looked up.

'You've seen someone?' asked Agatha.

Bobbie half chuckled in disbelief. She glanced down at the name and nodded.

'I'm not sure I can believe it and yet...'

She showed Agatha and Mary the name she'd found and explained the significance. It was still something of a long shot. Perhaps, it was a coincidence. The name was not so uncommon and yet Bobbie felt convinced it was the person they were after.

'The problem is, how do we prove it? Even if this person was over there at the battle, it doesn't mean that they stole the music, never mind killed two men.'

'True,' acknowledged Agatha who was eyeing her adopted niece, meaningfully.

Mary picked up on what was on Agatha's mind and said, 'It's a pity we don't have Harry here.'

'Who is Harry?' asked Bobbie, curious about what was passing between the two ladies.

The two ladies looked at each other for a moment as if reluctant to reveal what was on their minds. In fact, they were very reluctant to reveal what they were thinking, especially to the daughter of a senior policeman.

Bobbie was not about to let them away with this and pressed further.

'What is it that you don't want to tell me?' she asked, leaning forward and fixing her eyes on Mary.

Mary chuckled a little and shrugged. The cat was all but out of the bag anyway. They were all committed to the same cause: find the murderer of George Rankin and Matt Nicholls. How this was accomplished might raise an eyebrow, but the overall objective of finding justice for the two dead men was paramount.

'Harry was our former butler,' explained Mary. 'He has now joined the police and is working towards becoming a detective. Prior to the War, his profession was quite different and certainly wouldn't have suggested a career in law enforcement.'

'How do you mean?' asked Bobbie, now very curious.

'He was a burglar.'

Bobbie erupted into surprised laughter and then sat back in her chair as she considered the implications of what Mary was suggesting.

'Are you suggesting?'

'Yes,' said Mary and Agatha in unison.

'But...'

'It is unconventional I grant you,' admitted Agatha.

'Illegal you mean,' added Bobbie, although something in the tone of her voice suggested that the idea had not been rejected quite yet.

'True,' said Mary, 'but it's in a good cause. I mean you do want to bring the killer to justice?' Mary could have added a note towards Bobbie's own personal ambitions, but she felt that this would set the wrong tone.

Agatha pointed to the sheet music that they had borrowed from Sol Maxim.

'The only requirement is to enter the apartment and see if they can locate what Mr Maxim gave us.'

'Nothing else,' added Mary.

'Nothing else,' muttered Bobbie, slowly warming to the idea. Then a thought occurred to her.

'But you're not suggesting one of us break into the apartment, surely?'

Agatha licked her lips which was a habit of hers when she was about to impart an idea. She leaned forward.

'Well, as it happens, when Mary and I went to the precinct, to meet that young man of yours...,' said Agatha.

'He's not my young man,' pointed out Bobbie, bristling slightly.

'Yes, yes I'm sure he's not,' said Mary with a grin that a Cheshire cat would have deemed sly.

Agatha pressed on, 'Anyway, while we were waiting in the entrance of the precinct Mary and I ended up chatting with a young man who may have just the skills we need. However, I'm not sure how we can contact him.'

'I think I may be able to help there,' said Bobbie, smiling, despite her reservations, at the scheme Agatha and Mary had conceived.

'That's the spirit, Bobbie,' exclaimed Agatha which gave Bobbie a flush of pride. Then a thought struck Agatha. She turned towards Ella-Mae and said, 'I think we may need you to do a small job for us this afternoon. I hope you don't mind.'

Ella-Mae adored Agatha. She, herself, was closer to seventy than sixty, but could easily have passed for half that. She smiled at Agatha and said, 'Name it, Lady Frost.'

27

Lindy's on 50th street, at six in the evening, was full of the Broadway crowd enjoying a pre-theatre meal or lining their stomachs before hitting the speakeasies. The two young ladies caused their usual stir amongst the men who, at this time, comprised a mixture of journalists, politicians and mobsters. The acting folk, at least those who had jobs, were at their theatres, but would appear later.

Bobbie saw Damon Runyon at his usual table. His company was rather unusual. Bobbie recognised a pitcher from the New York Yankees and, rather worryingly, given his past connection with fixing baseball matches, Arnold Rothstein.

Bobbie, followed by the ladies, marched over to Runyon's table. The arrival of the ladies caused the gentlemen all to rise from their seats before shuffling along to allow the ladies to sit down and join them.

'Miss Flynn,' said Rothstein, 'what a pleasure it is to meet you again. And who, may I ask, are your friends?'

Introductions were made by Bobbie, which caused no end of delight, on the part of the head of the Jewish organised crime syndicate to meet a real-life lady. The pitcher, meanwhile, made a different kind of pitch towards Mary, but struck out quite quickly.

'I am understanding, Red, that you are needing this gentleman's help again?' asked Runyon.

'I am, Mr Rothstein. Perhaps Lady Frost may explain.'

The three gentlemen turned in the direction of Agatha, who proceeded to shock.

'On a recent expedition to Midtown North precinct, I met a charming young man by the name of 'Lefty' Mulligan. Do you perhaps know this gentleman?'

'I am not personally acquainted, your ladyship,' said Rothstein nobly. 'You say charming?' The 'Lefty' that Rothstein knew of had probably never been called this in his life and might have ripped the shirt off the back of anyone that would impugn his criminal credentials, in such a carefree manner.

'Why yes,' said Agatha. 'I found him most interesting. He told me about several jobs he'd pulled off without the police having the least idea as to who was responsible. I am sure his mother must be very proud of his proficiency in his chosen career.'

The three men's mouths were all hanging open by this stage. But Agatha hadn't finished, not by a long way.

'You do not want us to pull 'Lefty' in and teach him a lesson?' asked Rothstein.

'Oh no, nothing like that,' replied Agatha, before turning to a waitress who had just arrived and was taking orders for drinks again for all the table. The drinks in question were Gin Rickeys.

'I like your friends, Damon,' said Rothstein, looking amused at the journalist. 'Full of surprises.'

'You are telling me?' replied Runyon drily.

'As I was saying,' continued Agatha, 'we need 'Lefty' to pull a job for us.'

The timing of this request was unfortunate for the baseball pitcher as he had just drained the rest of his gin. It prompted a coughing fit from the Yankees' finest pitcher and laughter in his two male friends. When calm had returned to the table, Rothstein studied Agatha very closely.

'I do not normally ask why people want things. I appreciate that this is not my business. I hope you will appreciate my position here in asking, on behalf of Mr Mulligan, why he needs to put himself at risk in such a manner.'

'You may, of course. I would like to reiterate that this is not being done for personal gain. You should see it as intelligence gathering,' said Agatha. Then she turned to Bobbie and said, 'Perhaps you would care to enlighten Mr Rothstein.'

Bobbie nodded and briefly outlined the background to their desire to have 'Lefty' gain entry to the apartment, in a manner that the law tended to take a dim view of. When Bobbie had finished telling the story of Rankin and Nicholls, Rothstein shook his head.

'Well, once more, Miss Flynn, you have uncovered a story that disturbs me greatly. Two young men who go to France to fight for their country only to lose their lives here is very sad indeed. I am happy to help bring this affair to a conclusion, even if it does generally go against my principles to help the police, you understand.'

'We understand,' said Bobbie.

'I promise you that 'Lefty' will assist you in this matter. Do you have the address that he must enter?'

'We have someone working on this right as we speak,' said Agatha.

Ella-Mae watched her quarry climb up the steps to the apartment on 97th street, near the turn to Madison Avenue. By any standards, this was a rather upmarket apartment block. Ella-Mae instructed the cab driver to wait while she exited the cab and went to check on the address of the person she was following.

Mission accomplished, she returned to the cab and soon she was speeding off to Lindy's where she had arranged to meet Agatha, Mary and Bobbie. She hoped that they were still there. Sometimes it was difficult for a woman of colour to enter some establishments and her fear was that this would be one of them. Even hailing a cab was fraught with difficulty. Thankfully, Mary had helped in this matter by doing this for her and then handing the cab driver ten dollars with the instruction that he was to take Ella-Mae wherever she requested.

Arriving at Lindy's, she saw that the establishment did not have a colour bar. She walked in, but still felt mildly self-conscious. She scanned the diners for Agatha and Mary. Then she saw Bobbie waving over at her. This was a relief. She headed straight over to the table but remained standing. Then the three men did something that shocked her.

They all stood up.

'This is Ella-Mae,' explained Agatha. 'She has been tailing our suspect this afternoon. I hope with success.'

All eyes turned to the little housekeeper.

'I have the address.'

Patrick 'Lefty' Mulligan was so named because, rather like Chubby Chadderton, he'd lost his hand during the War. Despite receiving a small pension from Uncle Sam for his service, 'Lefty' had decided that the skills he had spent refining prior to the War would hold him in good stead after hostilities had ended. He often boasted, away from the earshot of policemen, that there was no safe that could keep him out.

In this, he was as good as his word. As a result, he was gainfully employed by many of the gangs. His speciality was nothing so common as burglary and stealing silverware. That was at the lower end of the evolutionary scale, as far as 'Lefty' was concerned. He often said this, although, as a practicing Catholic, he was suspicious of any suggestion that he was descended from apes.

Cracksmen of 'Lefty's' calibre were a rare breed and he was in demand for obtaining important documents, often from lawyers' offices, which provided insight into criminal cases or, better still, removing incriminating evidence. On a few occasions his practice had extended to removing letters that might otherwise have proved embarrassing and expensive, in a few divorce cases.

All in all, 'Lefty' was independent, esteemed and industrious. Of course, such talent was never going to go, entirely, unnoticed by New York's finest. 'Lefty' was often called upon to appear at one precinct or another, to explain his whereabouts, on one evening or another, hence his encounter with Agatha. He took these requests in the spirit they were made. Both the police and 'Lefty' knew that there would always be some witness or another who could swear blind to the fact that the cracksman had been attending one charitable benefit or other function that evening.

So it was with no great alarm that 'Lefty' greeted a man, built like a heavyweight prize fighter, who placed a hand on his shoulder and informed him that Mr Rothstein requested his presence. The man in question was Lenny Choynski, an associate of Rothstein, whose chief job was to look threatening. Nature had bestowed upon him enough size and a face that only a mother could love, to ensure that he was an unqualified success in his chosen profession.

'Now?' asked 'Lefty'.

'Now,' confirmed Lenny.

28

97th Street near Madison, New York: 1st February 1922

It was a crowded cab.

Bobbie sat with Agatha, Mary, Ella-Mae and 'Lefty' Mulligan outside their quarry's apartment on 97th street. They watched as their quarry left, which resulted in Ella-Mae jumping out of the cab and acting as a tail. The group in the cab watched as they walked down the street until both arrived at a bus stop.

There was a nervous silence in the cab, at least from the ladies. 'Lefty' seemed a little more relaxed but, then again, this was his profession and for a few minutes work in the morning, he was about to earn one hundred bucks, which was a lot of scratch by any man's estimation.

He held in his hand a folder containing the sheet music borrowed from Sol Maxim. The job was clear, rather basic by his standards. He knew what he had to do. In one of the most unusual briefings he had ever experienced, or was ever likely to, he had met the three ladies along with Lenny Choynski at Lindy's. It was a good job that Lenny had been there, otherwise he was not sure he would have believed what he was being asked to do. When he heard, and then when he saw the fifty, he was in.

'Let's wait until they're both on the bus,' suggested Agatha. 'Then I'll go in and commence the first stage of the operation.'

The plan was simplicity in itself. Agatha would go into the apartment building acting as an interested party for renting a room. Quite why an obviously refined Englishwoman of a certain age would want to rent a one-bedroom apartment was hopefully not a question that the superintendent would dwell on.

As the superintendent took Agatha to view the room, Bobbie and Mary, with the help of 'Lefty' would gain access to the apartment in order to search it. There was no reason to suppose that the sheet music would be there, rather than in a safety deposit box, but all had agreed that their suspect would have no inkling that they were under investigation.

Silence fell once more upon the cab and then a bus appeared and drove past them. All eyes followed the bus until it stopped. Two minutes later it departed. The bus stop was empty.

'I think that's our cue,' announced Agatha. With that, she opened the door of the cab and hopped out. Looking both ways on the road she walked across to the apartment block.

'That's some dame,' said 'Lefty' from within the cab. There was going to be no disagreement from the two young women on that score. They watched as Agatha went inside and could see her chatting with the superintendent. The man appeared in front of the reception desk. He was rather overweight and only a little taller than Agatha, who was no Amazon herself. He was grinning like a schoolboy meeting a sporting hero.

As soon as he led her away, the three remaining occupants of the cab hopped out and crossed the road. They headed up the stairs, each offering a silent prayer that the empty apartment that Agatha was going to see was not on the same floor as their suspect.

They took the elevator to the third floor which was a mercy as Bobbie's ankle was giving her some pain. Stepping out of the elevator they were relieved to see that the corridor was free. They went to apartment 3005. As a precaution, Bobbie knocked on the door. The one thing that they did not know was if someone else lived there. This would, of course, derail any plan to conduct their search.

Bobbie gave two series of raps with her cane. No answer. Mary nodded to 'Lefty' who took a leather wallet out of his pocket and laid it down on the floor. He opened it out to reveal a number of implements that were varying levels of thickness as well as a couple of keys.

Kneeling, 'Lefty' assessed the type of lock he was facing. A smile broke out across his face. Such is the contagiousness of so simple an act, the two ladies were soon smiling with their burglar friend.

Extracting a long metal pin, 'Lefty' inserted it in the lock. In the blink of an eye, the ladies heard the most satisfying sound in the world at that moment. The sound of a lock clicking open.

They piled into the apartment. It was not large, but there was a sense of space in the living room. The furnishing was tasteful, rather minimal and in the art deco style. It was also spotless. The owner clearly had a neat mind. The only thing that made the three entrants pause was the cat sleeping on the sofa. It really was fast asleep because it made no stir as they walked into the main room.

Not wishing to wake the cat, Mary whispered, 'I'll take the bedroom and the bathroom.'

'Lefty' started to look behind the pictures in the apartment for a safe, while Bobbie attacked the bookcase and the drawers in the cabinet beside it.

'Sure is a lot of war memorabilia,' noted 'Lefty' as he saw the shelves filled with some medals, a German spike helmet and a British gas mask. This was not all; one wall had photographs of groups of soldiers together and one bullet-ridden French tricolour. On the bureau were two dozen bullets for a 1903 Springfield, pointing upwards set in a wooden plinth.

Bobbie looked at the assorted items. The impact was rather morbid. The room was clean and fresh yet the atmosphere was drenched in sadness. Bobbie tried to rid herself of the overwhelming sense of death and focus on the task they had come to accomplish. Find evidence related to the murders.

Five minutes of thorough searching had turned up nothing in the living room. The only place Bobbie and 'Lefty' had not looked was underneath the cat. Any decision on waking the cat was made rendered redundant when Mary reappeared.

Smiling.

Her two hands were behind her back. With a flourish, she threw her hands in the air. In one hand was a folder that clearly contained sheets of paper. In the other was something that gave Bobbie a jolt. It was a large, battered notebook with a leather cover. Mary saw Bobbie's eyes track towards it.

'Is that what I think it is?' asked Bobbie. There was a tremor in her voice and, for reasons she could barely fathom, tears stung her eyes. She felt 'Lefty's' one good hand grip her elbow.

'I'm sorry,' he said and he too was almost in tears at seeing a fallen comrade's work.

Mary brought over the notebook and opened it. Inside were notes with ideas for lyrics and sketched musical notations. There were at least fifty pages in the notebook. The last two dozen pages were fully worked up songs. Bobbie recognised a few of them from the show "*Heaven's Below*". As they did not feel there was much time, they did not dwell on this. The other folder's contents matched exactly the couple of sheets that Sol Maxim had pinched. There was no question that their suspect had simply transcribed these from the original notes.

One other question was finally answered.

It was Bobbie who gave a name to the true writer of the songs. She had seen the name written on the inside cover of the leather book.

'So, it was Oscar who wrote the songs. Oscar Horowitz,' said Bobbie in a whisper.

This was met with silence for a few seconds and then 'Lefty' spoke for all of them when he said with a voice brimming with anger and emotion, 'Buddy, you won't be forgotten. I promise you; you won't be forgotten.'

29

An aspect of amateur detectives' work that often goes unreported, in this elevated form of literature, is the fact that the hero often has a day job that must be done, in between making intuitive jumps that lead to the collaring of master criminals.

Having experienced the high of finding the final piece of proof needed to identify the killer of George Rankin and, probably, Matt Nicholls, Bobbie had to endure a day of unrelenting tedium, at least by comparison to the excitement faced earlier.

It is, perhaps, not quite a matter of science, but there is no question that time passes more slowly when you want to be in another place, with another person, doing something other than what you are engaged in at that moment.

The obituary that Bobbie was writing about Homer P. Caldecutt, an entrepreneur in the inspiring area of pig breeding, did not quite rouse her spirits as it surely would have on any other day. But pass the day it did, although at what cost to Bobbie's sanity, only time would tell.

When the clock struck five, Bobbie was out of her chair like Charlie Paddock when the starter's gun goes off in the hundred. Buckner Fanley barely looked up as she rushed from the office.

Waiting outside in a cab was Agatha and Mary. They headed back, immediately, to the Flynn house in Greenwich Village.

'Did you ask your father to meet us here?' asked Agatha, as Bobbie joined them in the cab.

'I left a message. They're usually pretty good at passing these along.'

'Good,' replied Agatha. 'We shall have to play this very carefully.'

'I agree,' said Bobbie. 'If he believes for one second that we entered that apartment. Gosh, I still can't believe I did this.'

'Nonsense child,' said Agatha dismissively. 'It was in a good cause. It's not as if we planted evidence. We had a theory and we needed to prove it. We did so. That is all that we need to know.'

'Still...' remarked Bobbie but left the sentence unfinished.

'So how should we do this?' asked Mary. 'It would be best if your father and Detective Nolan arrive at the conclusion independently.'

'Exactly,' agreed Agatha. 'I propose we show them what Chubby discovered and let them draw a conclusion on what must happen next. If your father is half the man I think he is, he will be on the phone to a friendly judge asking for a search warrant.'

'And if he doesn't?' asked Bobbie.

'We nudge him,' said Mary with a grin.

'We nudge him,' concurred Agatha.

Just after six in the evening, Inspector Flynn returned home, accompanied by Detective Nolan, to find a reception committee in the form of Bobbie, Agatha and Mary. Although he was rather curious about the evidence, that Bobbie claimed they had uncovered, he was never going to appear so, adopting instead his usual world-weary countenance, mixed with more than a hint of impatience. Bobbie was used to this by now and Agatha simply ignored his manner, so its impact was, sadly, more limited than he would have liked.

The two detectives trooped into the room and joined the ladies sitting around the oak dining room table. Mrs Garcia had kindly prepared some *tapas* snacks, whose aroma provided a comforting mood given the rather grisly subject matter that was to be discussed.

Flynn took his place beside Bobbie which meant that Nolan had to sit at the end of the table beside Agatha. This appeared to amuse Bobbie, but Nolan was acutely sensitive to showing any attention towards Flynn's daughter.

'Well, what's this evidence I hear you have?' asked Flynn, getting straight down to business, in a manner that immediately earned the approval of Agatha. A nod from Agatha and Bobbie launched into their prepared case.

'As you know, we have always believed there was a connection between George Rankin's death and the mysterious songwriter O. Bonaty. There was no evidence to support this, of course, it was a hunch. Since then, with the help of my English friends, we have uncovered more threads that tie Bonaty to Mr Rankin and to the alleged suicide of Mr Nicholls.'

Bobbie paused for a second, worried that this introduction might test the patience of her father. It probably was.

However, he was not going to publicly humiliate her, so she had some time to establish the fundamentals.

'But there are a few missing pieces. Firstly, who is O. Bonaty? If George Rankin and Matt Nicholls' accusations are to be believed, how did this person get hold of the songs that were then used in the show "*Heaven's Below*".'

'How indeed?' agreed Flynn. He was nodding to this but, Bobbie noted, the first sign of outward impatience, as his index finger began to tap on the table.

'Well, we now have that connection, dad,' said Bobbie, trying to resist any hint of triumph in her voice.

Flynn's eyes widened at this. However, he had been a cop too long to fall on his knees at the first piece of evidence that was handed on a plate to him.

'You may be able to connect someone to those poor soldiers, but it doesn't mean that they stole any songs never mind selling them to be used in a Broadway show.'

'True,' agreed Agatha, jumping in. She licked her lips before adding in a suggestion about how they should proceed. 'However, I think that this does provide enough evidence for you to be able to call a friendly judge and obtain a search warrant.'

'What have you got?' asked Flynn. He was too much of a hunter not to feel a mixture of excitement and, more worryingly, pride at the prospect of catching a murderer and the crucial role that his daughter had, potentially, played in this.

Agatha nodded to Mary who took out of her bag the communication from Chubby containing the list of names who had worked at the Bouleuse hospital. Flynn went to take the list, but Mary smiled and shook her head.

'I think it would be better if Detective Nolan looked first,' said Mary, handing the list to Nolan who had, thus far, remained silent.

Nolan glanced at Flynn and received a nod. He took the list and began to go through each name using his index finger. There was not a sound in the room as Nolan's eyes scrolled down the list on each page.

And then he saw it.

He stopped and murmured, 'You're kidding me.'

'What do you mean?' snapped Flynn impatiently. 'What have you seen?'

Nolan didn't answer Flynn immediately, he addressed Bobbie for the first time and asked, 'Is this...?'

Bobbie nodded and said, 'Yes, I think it is. Perhaps you should show father before he blows a gasket.'

This brought smiles onto the faces of the ladies at least. The two men ignored the jibe. Nolan showed the name that he'd picked out on the sheet.

'Who is this?' asked Flynn.

When Bobbie explained who it was, Flynn sat back in his seat and whistled.

'What are you going to do?' asked Agatha.

Flynn fixed his eyes on Agatha and replied, 'Speak to a judge friend of mine and get ourselves a search warrant.'

'Can I make one other suggestion?' added Agatha.

'Shoot,' said Flynn.

As tempting as this suggestion was, and the half-smile that flickered on Agatha's face was immediately picked up by Flynn and earned a half-smile in return, Agatha told the old detective how the next stage of the investigation should go.

With a sigh, Flynn agreed.

30

Jackson Theatre, New York: 2nd February 1922

'This is the first and last time I will ever do something like this,' snarled Flynn to the three ladies. He was in a foul mood but, as men for centuries had always done, he went with what he had been told to do by the womenfolk.

'It's necessary,' said Bobbie, smoothing an errant lapel on his suit before returning to leaning on her cane. She felt more like Charlie Chaplin but resisted twirling it.

'Why?' asked Flynn.

'In case Sergeant Yeats does not find anything,' said Bobbie. She knew he would but had felt this would be a good way of covering their tracks and potentially provoking their suspect into a misstep.

'And it's justice for those men who were murdered,' said Agatha. 'Justice will be seen to be done.'

'It feels corny. Like something from a dime novel,' snapped Flynn back.

Agatha, who had done this many times, felt affronted at such an accusation, but bit back her reply. She did not feel like some amateur detective in a corny dime novel.

'Don't be so grumpy,' said Bobbie. 'You're worse than usual.'

That had its usual impact on her father. His tone softened, even if the undercurrent of rebelliousness remained solidly in place.

'I feel like a fraud. I'm taking credit for your work,' muttered Flynn. Even to give voice to such a thought was quite a step forward for Bobbie and both she and her father knew it. It was an acknowledgement that she had helped solve the crime. She knew what it had cost her father to say this. His opposition to her being involved with the crime desk, remained, but he could not deny either her capability or the results she had obtained.

'Nonsense,' said Agatha, keen to put this to bed. Both you and Detective Nolan have been key in this. Young Nolan deserves to have some credit for all the work he did eliminating suspects and establishing the timeline of Rankin's last hours.'

This was true and Flynn knew it. The time had come for him to acknowledge any further bellyaching would not only be ungracious, but it would also risk him seeming more mean-spirited than he actually felt.

Bobbie saw the first signs of resignation in his eyes and she kissed his forehead. Meanwhile, Agatha was more forthright and gave a hearty, 'That's the spirit.'

And so, Flynn walked out onto the stage to face an assembled crowd of friends of the deceased men, witnesses and suspects. He could not do so without one parting shot to the three ladies who were in the wings.

'At least none of the precinct are here to witness this,' said Flynn through the side of his mouth before planting a cigar there and walking on ahead before any of the ladies could reply.

Detective Nolan was about to follow Flynn out when he glanced at Bobbie and frowned, his eyes directed towards the injured ankle and the cane.

Bobbie rolled her eyes and said for what was probably the fiftieth time, 'Softball accident.' This seemed to amuse the young detective which sent Bobbie's temper gauge rising. 'My batting average is probably not far off Babe Ruth's.'

This brought a raised eyebrow and then Nolan followed his boss onto the stage but walked along the side and then the back to sit among the assembled audience in the back row along with a couple of patrolmen.

The stage was full of people, all of whom were connected with the case. They sat in a semi-circle formed of three rows. Sitting in the front and middle was George Rankin's older brother. His face, like many of the others there, betrayed his confusion and even anxiety at what he was about to hear. Alongside him were a few band members that Rankin had played with, as well as Lucia Montez and the Amazonian figure of Louella LaForge. Desi Monterey sat on the other side of Miss LaForge. He was wearing a yellow Hawaiian shirt and white trousers. Life was his performance, not just singing.

On the row behind, Ben Strauss sat beside two representatives from Leo Feist's Music Publishers, Nick Jones and Miss Summer. To their right, were other musicians who had worked with Matt Nicholls. At the end of the row were two people connected to the show being staged in the theatre, Herman Moss, the producer and Omar Maltbie III who had written the book of the show. At the end of the row was Janice Griffith, the star of the show.

Flynn took a few moments to survey the gathering. Everyone was there who needed to be there, either as a witness or as a suspect. He wondered how Detective Yeats was getting on with Grimm and O'Riordan. He'd sent them to search the flat that, unknown to him, Bobbie had visited already. It was one of the biggest gambles of his career. He felt his breathing quickening at the thought of how it could all go up in smoke if they failed to turn up anything.

Then, as if it were a *coup de theatre*, he saw Yeats appear in the opposite wings with Grimm and the fat oaf, O'Riordan. The captain gave a nod, but Flynn's eyes were on Yeats. There was a satisfied smile on his face as he held up a leather-bound item in his hand. All of this went unnoticed by the people seated before Flynn.

It was time to begin.

'My name is Inspector Flynn of the NYPD. You may be wondering why the New York Police Department has called you together at short notice,' said Flynn. 'Especially here, to a theatre on Broadway. This theatre, as you'll have seen outside, plays host to the show, "*Heaven's Below*". Can't say I've seen it myself, but I gather from Mr Moss it's a good show. Although perhaps Mr Moss is biased. He produces it.'

This brought good-natured laughter from the assembled group and eased the, undeniable, tension on the stage.

'We're here because of one, possibly two murders that may be connected to the show.'

Herman Moss stood up at this, 'I say Inspector Flynn, you know you just can't throw things like that around. It could be very damaging, sir.'

Flynn held his hands up, in order to placate the producer. There was probably some truth in this.

'I agree sir,' replied Flynn, 'However, I think you may find that what I have to say will have the opposite affect and right a great wrong. If you're half the man I think you are, you'll figure out how to help your show and see justice done.'

Bobbie almost applauded how her father had not only dodged an awkward situation with great finesse, but also managed to make Herman Moss an ally with an appeal that engaged the producer's conscience, as well as his desire to keep the box office tills singing.

Flynn turned to Omar Maltbie III. The man was certainly every bit as large as Bobbie had suggested. He seemed to take up two seats.

'Mr Maltbie, if I may check, you created the show around the songs that were given to you, is that so?'

'It is,' replied Maltbie, investing the two words with great gravitas.

'Did you have much contact with the song writer at any point?'

'No, sir,' said Maltbie, with a dignified air, as if consorting with songwriters was beneath him.

Flynn spun around to Ben Strauss.

'Mr Strauss, you represent Bonaty. Yet, I'm right in thinking you've never met this person in your life.'

'Correct, Inspector,' confirmed Strauss.

Flynn's eyes flicked over towards Nick Jones from Leo Feist Inc. He was, as ever, sporting a tweed jacket, with a yellow bow tie, this time. Flynn didn't have to ask the question. Jones took the pipe from his mouth and grinned.

'Same goes for me, Inspector,' said Jones.

Flynn nodded at this and then made a great play in surveying the audience.

'It is our belief that the mysterious O. Bonaty not only stole the songs that have been used in the show but is also responsible for the murder of two men who knew that this had happened and tried to prove it.'

Jones and Strauss were on their feet immediately. They looked at one another and then Jones sat down, deferring to the lawyer's greater experience in cross-examination.

'Say, Inspector, that's a mighty big accusation. Big accusations need mighty big pieces of evidence to support it,' said Strauss with a smile that did not disguise the threatening undertone.

'We'll come to that Mr Strauss. Perhaps such an accusation might have your client coming out of the woodwork.'

'I hardly think that is either appropriate police work or, frankly, in any way relevant to your job.'

'Let me be the judge of that,' replied Flynn, amiably. He was beginning to enjoy his moment in the spotlight, particularly as he could see O'Riordan looking impatient to make an arrest.

'I shall explain myself and then, perhaps, all will be clear.'

Strauss nodded and sat down.

'George Rankin and Matt Nicholls were in the same platoon during the War. We found a photograph in Mr Rankin's apartment which showed him with four other men, all holding musical instruments, all in army uniform. One of those men was Matt Nicholls who, it is alleged, committed suicide just before Christmas. He had suffered from depression since the War and was known to be an alcoholic. It fits that he took his own life. Or so we have been led to think. We believe that Rankin and Nicholls probably played in a band with the three other men in the photograph. For the record, they were named Oscar, Lance and Archie.'

Flynn now had the group spellbound by the story. No one said anything. All were intent on finding out what had happened to these men and how it was connected to the show and the murders.

'Three of the men, Lance Graham, Archie Wilde and Oscar Horowitz were killed on the first day of the German offensive at Marne on 15th July 1918. Mr Rankin and Mr Nicholls were the only survivors from this group, but both were wounded. We know that they ended up in hospital, at Bouleuse, before they were transferred to different sites.'

Flynn paused to let this sink in. Five men who had served their country, three of whom had not made it back. The detective glanced towards Nick Jones, who had also gone over to France. There was sadness etched over his face. Flynn, immediately, felt sympathy for the man.

'Before his death, Mr Nicholls went to Ben Strauss and Leo Feist. He accused the enigmatic Bonaty of plagiarism. His claims were ignored.'

Jones was on his feet again, but Flynn motioned for him to sit down. He was either getting tired of being interrupted or was enjoying the speech too much. Probably, a bit of both.

'They were ignored for good reasons, I'm sure. Lots of people like to jump on the bandwagon and claim credit for books or songs that weren't created by them. Sometimes they can spook the true creators or publishers enough to extort some money from them. In some cases, their claim is true.'

Jones stayed on his seat, but called out, 'Can you prove this Inspector?'

Flynn smiled and his eyes flicked, once more to the wings, where he saw the reassuring sight of the battered leather notebook in the hands of Detective Yeats. He hoped to hell it contained what he thought it did.

'We'll come to that. Let me finish the story,' replied Flynn. 'We can only speculate on what happened next. We know that Rankin and Nicholls saw one another, isn't that so? Miss Montez.'

Many heads turned towards the attractive singer. She nodded reluctantly.

'What happened with Mr Rankin after he and Nicholls met up? Miss Montez?'

A little reluctantly at first, and then with more belief, she replied, 'He was angry. Very angry. I'd never seen him like this before.'

'And when Mr Nicholls died, soon after you'd met him?' probed Flynn.

'George changed. He was afraid. And angry. He became...' Miss Montez paused at this moment, as she searched for the right word. 'He became a little crazy. I didn't like what I was seeing. I told him to see a doctor. He wouldn't listen...'

'Thanks, Miss Montez,' said Flynn in a soothing voice. 'Yes, he was angry and probably afraid. He knew that his friend hadn't committed suicide and he knew why someone would want to kill him. Would they do the same to him, if he continued to press the case, started by Mr Nicholls, that this Bonaty had stolen the work of another man? We know now he was right.'

'Prove it,' called out Jones once more.

'He's right,' said Ben Strauss. 'This is just a story, without a shred of evidence.'

'That's where you are wrong, Mr Strauss. Mr Jones, you too. We do have evidence. But let me continue the story. I think we should go back to that awful day in France when the Germans began their offensive. I cannot begin to imagine the fear they must have felt when the bombardment began. Mr Jones, perhaps you'll know.'

Jones' face was a mask. It was if he was fighting a battle against his emotions, his memories. He nodded and wiped away tears that had formed in his eyes.

'I apologise, Mr Jones. Those memories can only be of the most terrible kind. So many men lost their lives that day, including Lance Graham, Archie Wilde and Oscar Horowitz. One of these men was the true creator of these songs. Again, we can only speculate as to what happened next. Their bodies were collected and buried while the two survivors, Rankin and Nicholls made it to the hospital at Bouleuse. And this is where our friend O. Bonaty enters the picture. Only Bonaty, as I'm sure you all suspect, is not the real name.'

Flynn paused at that moment while he let this sink in.

'It is an anagram. I'll save you the trouble of trying to work it out. It stands for, "Not a boy",' announced Flynn.

There were gasps from the group.

'Yes, Bonaty is a woman. And a killer. During the War, this person was a nurse at the Bouleuse hospital. Over this time, I have no doubt she did her job as a nurse in the most trying of circumstances. But she also used this time to separate many men from their possessions. She was a thief. We have a name for this type of illness: kleptomania. This nurse was a kleptomaniac. She took a notebook of songs from either Nicholls or Rankin; they had probably been added mistakenly to their belongings. She took them as she took many other things from that hospital and then brought them home, after the War was over. I mean who would think to search the possessions of a young woman who, in any other sense, should be considered a hero.'

Silence greeted this. No one spoke now.

'Yes, this woman was a hero. But, like the men who served, she was just one of thousands. Anonymous. Unrewarded. Such is war. In many respects, she would have my sympathy. But no. That can't be. She chose instead to try her luck and sell the songs. And against all odds, it worked. Of course, she was smart. She made sure that these songs found their way to the right publisher. More than that, she began to date the very man who would make their success assured.'

There was a shout of "no" from the audience. All eyes turned to the man standing.

Nick Jones stared down at his secretary Miss Summer.

'Beth is this true?' demanded Jones.

'It is true, Jones,' said Flynn. 'We know that Miss Summer was a nurse at Bouleuse in 1918.'

Tears streamed down the face of the young woman. She seemed to be in such shock that it was difficult to believe that she was the killer that Flynn was claiming she was.

'It's not true,' snarled Jones turning to Flynn. His face was almost savage in its hatred towards the inspector.

At this point, the stage echoed to the footsteps of Captain Frank O'Riordan. He'd taken the leather notebook from Yeats, who tried not to burst out laughing and failed. O'Riordan stomped onto the stage, brandishing the notebook. With a cigar planted between his teeth, his hat lying back on his head and a belly flopping over the waist of his trousers, he looked every inch what a police captain should look like.

'Here's your proof here,' said O'Riordan, waving the notebook around. This was just about his first involvement in the case and he was going to make damn sure that he was the one who made the collar.

Like many things in his life, he would regret it.

He strode forward and opened the notebook. It was just about possible to make out the scribbled musical notes and ideas for lyrics.

'We searched this woman's apartment this morning. We found this and a good deal else besides. She has an armoury up there that Uncle Sam would be very interested in.'

O'Riordan was now alongside Jones and towering over the sobbing Miss Summer. He handed the notebook to Jones.

'Look for yourself,' he snarled at Jones before addressing Miss Summer. 'You are coming with me.'

He put his hand on the shoulder of the young woman. Miss Summer nodded and rose meekly from her seat.

What happened next shocked everyone.

In a movement that was as fast as it was unexpected, she pulled an object from her pocket and held it beside O'Riordan's head. It was green and just about the size of a large pear only a little deadlier.

It was a grenade.

A grenade she had stolen from a dead soldier and smuggled back home. It was grenade from her collection of deadly weapons that had sailed home on the *Aquitania*, unchecked because, as Inspector Flynn had said, *who would check a nurse's baggage?*

O'Riordan's eyes widened when he saw the grenade, flicking between the deadly intent in Miss Summer's eyes to the anger in Inspector Flynn's. This had not been a good idea, he concluded. Not a good idea at all.

And then things got worse. Particularly for Francis O'Riordan.

Miss Summer, with her free hand, removed the pin of the grenade that was now brushing his cheek. He felt the cold metal and it made him shiver. At least, that's what he tried to convince himself had happened.

In a voice that was quiet, yet still managed to carry across the stage she said, nervously, 'If anyone tries anything, we all die.'

31

The removal of the pin triggered several things - loud screams for one thing and that was just from Desi Monterey, as well as a near bowel movement from Omar Maltbie III. He sat down, crossed his legs and prayed that the nightmare would end soon without his bulky form decorating the expanse of the Jackson Theatre.

The collective shock of Miss Summer's deadly move was somewhat diluted by Desi's emotional breakdown. It needed Louella LaForge to pull him back to reality. This took an unusual form. Rather than a few gentle slaps around the face to distract his attention, she landed a vicious uppercut, into his solar plexus. In Nolan's judgement, it would have given most heavyweight prize fighters something to ponder on from their position spread-eagled on the canvas.

This was quite shocking, in itself, but at least it had the virtue of, quite literally, knocking the wind out of Desi's screams. Flynn resisted the impulse to applaud, while Miss LaForge merely shrugged and uttered a rather unconvincing apology.

Apart from Desi's gasps for air, there was no noise now as everyone tried to rationalise how the stand-off would play out.

Flynn was the first to speak.

'Miss Summer,' he began. He was old school enough to believe that even with deadly murderers, politeness was the first and best option before more aggressive tones were employed. 'Surely you can't think you can escape from all this. It's over.'

'Not necessarily,' said Miss Summer. And to give her some credit, Flynn did not discount the possibility that she could pull off some form of escape. However, her method was entirely unexpected.

Perhaps it was the much vaunted, but scientifically unproven, concept of 'female intuition', but Miss Summer had quickly understood a number of things, while Inspector Flynn was speaking. It had struck her when, by chance, she had seen Bobbie standing in the wings.

This was the person who was responsible for her downfall. Of this, she was absolutely certain. The next thought that struck her was the name. In her role as a secretary at Leo Feist Inc, she had developed an acute memory for names. And the young woman's name rang a bell. Rather loudly, in fact.

Roberta Flynn.

Was it a coincidence that the senior policeman in front of her was related? He'd given his name as Flynn. It seemed the apple did not fall far from the tree. She fixed her eyes on the wings and found herself staring directly at Bobbie.

'Miss Flynn, please come over here,' said Miss Summer.

'Don't move,' ordered Inspector Flynn to his daughter.

'Inspector Flynn, if Miss Flynn does not come over here, immediately, then I promise that you will have the blood of, at least, a dozen people on your hands.'

'Bobbie don't,' urged Flynn, not for the first time in his life. And, not for the first time, she ignored what he said. To his horror, he heard her footsteps echo behind him. He snapped at her, 'What do you think you're doing?'

Bobbie was now standing directly in front of Miss Summer and a heavily perspiring Captain O'Riordan. It's odd, the things you think about, as you are standing facing certain death. For example, some peoples' lives flash before them, for others it's a sudden desire to eat a hotdog, or, in Bobbie's case, it was the thought that this would forever confirm in her father's eyes that he did not want her anywhere near the crime desk.

'Move,' said Miss Summer to O'Riordan, who, for once, was happy to take orders from a woman. Then Miss Summer looked around her and said, 'All of you. Move out of the way unless you really want to be blown to bits.' All the while she had her eyes fixed on Bobbie.

There was a low noise of shoes scraping on the floor of the stage as the assembled audience shuffled away from Miss Summer.

All except one person.

Detective Nolan was standing directly behind Miss Summer now. His eyes flicked down to Bobbie's leg, which made her wonder why he was checking her out at such a dangerous moment. Men were unbelievable sometimes. Then she realised what he had in mind.

'Now Miss Flynn, you and I are going to exit stage left. If anyone tries anything stupid, Inspector Flynn, your daughter will be dead.'

'So will you,' pointed out Flynn. Like O'Riordan, he was perspiring heavily now. Every nightmare he'd ever had about his daughter being involved with crime was coming true just then and he cursed himself for the folly he had agreed to.

'If I go with you, it'll be the chair for me anyway. I suspect this will be a little quicker,' replied Miss Summer coldly.

Bobbie's heart was racing like a jackrabbit being chased by wild dogs. Her hand slipped down the stem of the cane while her eyes remained fixed on Miss Summer. Then she saw Detective Nolan nod out of the corner of her eye.

Bobbie took one step back. Miss Summer frowned. This was not supposed to be what happened. Seconds later, she felt a powerful hand push her forward. The grenade slipped from her hand and fell to the floor, with a clatter that in the silence of the theatre felt like it was echoing up and down Broadway.

Bobbie flipped the cane so that the handle was on the floor, rather like a hockey stick. With a flick of her wrists, she slipped the grenade into the orchestra pit.

'Duck,' shouted Flynn, but it was clear that the people on the stage were all too aware of the action they had to take.

A second or two passed where all that could be heard was the whimpering of Desi Monterey and Omar Maltbie III.

The explosion was shocking in its suddenness. And then it was over. Bits of wood and metal flew upwards into the air and landed on the stage with a clank and a thud. Bobbie kept her head covered in case anything heavy landed on her, but it was all over in the blink of an eye. She looked up and saw that Detective Nolan was on top of a squirming Miss Summer. He was joined by the two hefty patrolmen. Pinned thus, Miss Summer's struggles soon gave way to sobbing.

Within seconds, Bobbie felt two hands take her arm. It was her father.

'Bobbie are you all right?' he asked looking her up and down.

Bobbie sketched a smile and nodded; still not sure she could trust her voice. She hugged her father and said, 'Don't worry. I'm fine.'

They were joined a few moments later by Agatha and Mary. Bobbie was embraced by Mary.

Meanwhile Agatha and Flynn's eyes met. There was no ignoring the anger in a father's eyes and Agatha wisely said nothing. It was only fair that Flynn said his piece.

'I hope you're happy,' he said in low, angry voice. 'I suppose this was your idea. Well, it could have got us all killed. I don't know what possessed me to go along with this.'

Agatha said nothing to this, there was nothing she could say. It was both true and unfair, but this was not the time to discuss such nuances, with a man who was tired, afraid and relieved in equal measure.

Seeing that Agatha would not respond, Flynn put on his hat, shook his head and left her standing with Bobbie and Mary. He headed towards Miss Summer whose arms were now locked by the two patrolmen, one of whom was placing handcuffs on her wrists.

Miss Summer half-smiled when she saw Flynn standing before her. It took all the self-control he barely knew he had, not to attack her. His hatred for her was so real he could almost touch it.

'You were right about one thing,' snarled Flynn in a voice that was barely above a whisper. 'The chair will take a lot longer to kill you.'

The smile left Miss Summer's face and she was led away by the two patrolmen. Flynn watched her leave the stage and then he saw Bobbie, accompanied by the two ladies, who were helping her walk, heading off in the opposite direction.

'Where are you off to now?' shouted Flynn in exasperation at his departing daughter.

Bobbie stopped and grinned at her father.

She said, 'Sorry daddy, I have a story to post.'

32

It was a little after twelve in the afternoon when Bobbie limped up the staircase of the Tribune building that led to the second-floor offices of the *New York American*. Her arrival in the main office which housed mostly male news staff was always a moment to savour for those present. The sight of Bobbie limping, however, was somewhat unusual leading almost inevitably to a few ribald comments.

'Hey Red,' shouted one wag, 'What happened to your ankle? Did you get that jumping off the wardrobe?' asked Ade Barton, the crime reporter.

Bobbie was used to these comments by now and could give as good as she got.

'You know what they say, Ade,' grinned Bobbie as she made her way through the desks, 'there's many a slip between cup and lip.'

This brought a roar of approval from the newsmen and was enough to have Thornton Kent out of his seat and to the door of his office, steam pouring from his ears. Bobbie pushed past him and went straight inside to his office. Kent was completely bewildered by this, not the least because Bobbie had asked for the morning off.

'What do you want?' he said, glaring at her. This was his normal manner of dealing with newsmen and he saw no reason to alter it when dealing with a young woman.

'The front page,' said Bobbie.

This was, to say the least, a refrain that he was used to hearing, was sick of hearing and made him long for the day that a member of his team would walk inside and politely request two column inches somewhere in the middle of the paper. He rolled his eyes and gave his usual reply to such a request.

'Get the hell out of my office,' snapped Kent waving at her dismissively, but there was just a hint of hesitancy in there too. Bobbie had delivered two scoops in the first few weeks of 1922. Did she have another? Something in the half-smile on her face suggested that she had.

Bobbie rose to her feet, put her two hands on the desk and leaned over him. There were probably worse things in the world for Kent to be looking at just then and Bobbie was aware of this.

'What would you say if I told you that I was there when the killer of George Rankin and Matt Nicholls was arrested today?'

'Matt who?' sneered Kent.

'And that the killer was none other than O. Bonaty, the songwriter of "*Heaven's Below*".'

Kent sat forward. She had his attention, now.

'Go on,' said Kent.

Bobbie sat down and quickly related not just the extraordinary events at the Jackson Theatre, but also the investigation and her role in it that led to the capture. She felt gratified by the fact that Kent not only listened, but asked questions to clarify some points as they went along. When she'd finished, he was silent for a few moments. Then he said, 'I want the story on my desk by three. Get out of here.'

A few hours later, Bobbie arrived home to an empty house. It was Mrs Garcia's night off, while her father was either still at the precinct with Miss Summer or with the Commissioner, receiving congratulations. After the thrill of the morning, followed by the triumph of the afternoon when Bobbie handed in her story to Kent, the feeling of energy pulsing through her set her mood spiralling as she sat in the empty house with no one to share her elation with.

Yet, this was tempered by the knowledge that a conversation awaited her. She knew her father would not easily forget the sight of her standing beside Miss Summer, her life under threat from the grenade. The successful outcome could not possibly mask the risks she'd run throughout the case, right up until the final frightening moments.

Bobbie wondered what mood her father would be in. While the feeling of elation slowly evaporated in the darkness of her house, she suspected her father would have felt this way through much of the day.

It was a little after seven when she heard a key in the door and then his footsteps on the stairs. He arrived in the dark living room and was surprised.

'Bobbie? Are you here?'

'Yes,' said Bobbie, who had been lying on the sofa seeking solace from the pattering of rain on the window. She raised her head up so that it peeked over the top of the sofa.

Her father walked in and joined her on the sofa as Bobbie curled her legs away from the other side. They sat in silence for a minute listening to the rain.

'Are you angry?' asked Bobbie finally.

She could not see, but there were tears in her father's eyes. He shook his head and tried to find some control for his voice.

'No. I'm not angry,' said Flynn. The anger had been there but, like Bobbie's sense of triumph, it had slowly faded away leaving a gnawing emptiness. He shook his head again and wiped his eyes. Bobbie realised now that he had shed tears. She leaned over to him and hugged him.

'I'm sorry,' she said while trying to fight back her own tears.

'I can't lose you too, Bobbie. It would be too much. I couldn't bear it,' said Flynn and at once felt guilty for being so selfish. It was her life. Who was he to force her into a life that she did not want to live? He wished it could be easier.

'I know,' whispered Bobbie.

Nothing was said for a minute or two. They listened to the rain and the traffic and the distant sirens.

'And what about Violet?' asked Flynn. 'You want it all honey. I don't blame you. But it's too much. What if something happened to you? What would it do to her?'

Bobbie thought of Violet and her heart made a violent lurch. The little girl had bonded with her now. She knew that, if she asked, she would come and live with them. And she had to now. The situation had gone too far.

A change of subject was needed.

'What happened with Miss Summer?' asked Bobbie.

The question was greeted with relief by Flynn.

'She confessed,' said Flynn. 'It was as we suspected. She stole the songbook from the belongings of Matt Nicholls. She thinks that they were picked up by the medics who collected the two men and were mistakenly given over to Nicholls. After the War she left nursing and was looking for work. She did a secretarial course and enjoyed it enough to look for something in that field. The job at Leo Feist Inc was her first after the War. That's when the idea to try and sell the songs came to her. She copied out the songs that she could see from the leather book and gave them to Sol Maxim. He played them to Feist and Jones who both liked what they heard. As she was like a gatekeeper for mail, she made up the name Bonaty and contacted Ben Strauss to represent her anonymously.

'You're saying that Mr Strauss never knew it was Miss Summer?' asked Bobbie.

'No. Strauss was telling the truth when he said he'd never met Bonaty. Anyway, Feist's are a major source of songs for Broadway and this is where Herman Moss enters the picture. He heard the songs and loved them. So now the songs were going to be in a show and that meant a lot of money potentially. It took nearly a year before the show made it onto the stage. At some point, Matt Nicholls saw the show and he recognised the songs. He sent letters to Leo Feist but, of course, Miss Summer made sure that they never reached either Feist or Jones. He went to Ben Strauss who threw him out. Then Nicholls came to the offices to try and see Feist. Miss Summer stopped him, but at this point, and she is very attractive, she managed to form a relationship with Nicholls. They met a few times and then, one morning after she had spent the night with him, she killed him in his room and made it seem like a suicide.'

'Oh my, how terrible,' said Bobbie.

'Now, she thought the matter was over, especially as the police had accepted the idea that Nicholls, who we know was a depressive, had taken his own life. She couldn't believe it when one of the firm's own song pluggers began to ask questions.'

'And so she did the same again,' said Bobbie.

'Yes. She had an affair with Rankin which made him break it off with Miss Montez. Then one morning, after she had spent the night with Rankin, she killed him.'

'But how did she ever escape without Mr Laszlo seeing her either arrive or leave?'

'I think that Rankin sealed his own fate on the former, but the latter was clever planning by Miss Summer,' said Flynn. 'Rankin helped sneak Miss Summer in when Laszlo was distracted. Then she spent the night with him. She had brought an old army revolver with her, one that she had filched from a dead officer at Bouleuse. She killed Rankin while he slept. using a pillow to muffle the sounds.'

'Poor Mr Rankin. But how did she escape?'

'The morning of the murder was one in which the cleaner, Lucy Deng, was due to come to the building. She had brought along clothes and a hat similar to what the cleaner wore. She simply walked out of the building disguised as the cleaner. No one would question a cleaner. Let's face it, hardly anyone notices them. Diabolical, but clever. So, she walked away, free. Her problems were, pending the police investigation of the murder, all but over. Except for one thing that she had not counted on.'

'What was that?' asked Bobbie.

Flynn sighed and rose from the sofa. He looked down at his daughter with a mixture of pride and weary sadness.

'You my dear,' said Flynn. 'She didn't count on someone like you making the connection between Rankin and Bonaty.

Epilogue

Chelsea Piers, New York: 3rd February 1922

It was that time in the morning that was neither dark nor light, but there was still a February-sized chill in the air at Chelsea Piers. Half-asleep passengers sullenly boarded the RMS Aquitania under umbrellas that shielded them from a soft rain falling sorrowfully on the harbour.

Bobbie had turned up with, much to her surprise, Flynn to say 'farewell' to their English friends: Kit and Mary Aston and Agatha. Given how Flynn and Agatha had parted the previous day, Bobbie was not the only one who was surprised by her father agreeing to join her on the dock.

Flynn, himself, was unsure what had motivated this desire to see this unusual English family off. Perhaps it was a desire to make sure that they really had left. He said as much to Bobbie, gruffly, over breakfast, but Bobbie was having none of that. She could tell when her father was lying and this was a whopper. She didn't push him on it. That he had said something to Agatha the previous morning was abundantly clear, but her ears had been ringing from the blast of the grenade so she could not hear. But she had the memory of the look on her father's face.

Anger.

Something in his manner over breakfast suggested there would not be a repeat of what he'd said the previous morning.

The morning that she might have been killed. The morning they all might have been killed.

Bobbie had not slept well that night. Perhaps it was the delayed shock of what had happened. Or perhaps it was the conversation with her father that evening when she'd seen him shed tears and the folly of her actions became all too clear.

Bobbie suspected that he would want to see Kit Aston off. He'd enjoyed his day's golfing the previous weekend with him and his uncle, Alastair. Kit's uncle had already left with Ella-Mae for San Francisco earlier in the week.

Kit received a hug from Bobbie and a peck on the cheek, as did Mary and Agatha.

As Mary released Bobbie from her hug she whispered in her ear, 'Let me know how it goes with that detective.'

Bobbie frowned, reddened and glanced to the side to see if her father had heard Mary. As it was, Flynn and Kit were chatting amiably before a handshake and a nod was deemed sufficient farewell between them.

Mary joined Kit on the gangway that led up to the first-class deck on the Aquitania. Bobbie gave Agatha a hug. There were tears in her eyes now for she knew she would miss Mary and this extraordinary woman.

Bobbie stood back from Agatha and went closer to the dockside to see Kit and Mary go up the gangway. She also wanted to give her father and Agatha privacy to make their peace.

She hoped.

Flynn and Agatha turned towards one another.

'I'm surprised to see you here,' said Agatha, getting straight to the point as ever. This brought a half-smile to Flynn's face.

'You're not the only one,' muttered Flynn sulkily.

'Did Bobbie put a gun to your head?' suggested Agatha wryly.

'At least it wasn't a grenade.'

Agatha's eyes widened at this, then she broke out into a smile. So did Flynn. He looked up at Kit and Mary waving down at Bobbie and felt a surge of an emotion that he could not quite identify.

'I owe you an apology,' said Flynn.

'No, you don't,' snapped Agatha.

Flynn's eyes flared in anger, 'Look lady, would you just keep quiet and let me speak.'

Agatha said nothing to this, which took Flynn by surprise. He paused a moment, as if waiting for some acerbic remark which did not come.

'Fine,' said Flynn. 'I was out of order and don't say anything, Lady Frost. Let me speak. I don't know what to do about Bobbie. I can't face the idea of her...of what she did yesterday. I blamed you, but the plain fact is whether you were here or not, she would have done what she did. Anyway, you were not to blame and I was wrong.'

Agatha listened intently, as she always did when someone she respected was speaking. Finally, when it seemed as if Flynn had said his piece, she spoke.

'You have nothing to apologise for,' said Agatha. 'Any father would have felt what you felt yesterday and I was partly responsible no matter what you say. Partly. The truth you will have to face is that your daughter is rather remarkable. She has a natural intuition for your profession and I have absolutely no doubt where it comes from.'

Flynn looked away. He hated praise for himself as much as he loved to hear it about his daughter.

'She wants it all, Lady Frost. She wants to be my daughter; she wants to be a mother to a young girl. She wants to be a reporter on the crime desk and solve crimes.'

'Would it be so bad to let her have what she wants? We both know life gives you too short a time to have the energy to accomplish the things you want to accomplish.'

'She can't have it all,' retorted Flynn.

'She's a woman,' pointed out Agatha sharply. 'She's not allowed to have it all.'

This jab caught Flynn in the solar plexus and he could detect the anger lurking beneath the remark. He knew it wasn't aimed at him. He knew she was talking about something so much bigger. He looked into her eyes.

She was unquestionably the smartest woman he had ever met. Those eyes burned with intelligence. And anger too. What had she been in her life? What could she have been had she been a man? Suddenly, he felt ashamed. Not for what he had done, although he knew he had some cause, but for what society had denied not just to this woman, but to all women. It was what he was doing to his own daughter. And he had justified it to himself as protecting her. What a fool he was.

Flynn nodded to Agatha and then his eyes flicked towards the liner. Agatha smiled and said, 'Yes, I probably should. I think you'll be glad to see the back of us.'

Flynn chuckled at this and said, 'I suspect you're right. I'll miss you too, Lady Frost. Will you be back?'

A sadness appeared in Agatha's eyes.

'I'm not sure. I'm not getting any younger. Goodbye Flynn.'

Agatha turned and walked up the ramp without looking back.

'Goodbye Lady Frost,' whispered Flynn.

You like him, don't you. He's a dreamboat.

Out of the mouths of children, thought Bobbie. And then she wondered what she was doing for the hundredth time in the last ten minutes. What she was doing at that moment was standing under an umbrella outside Midtown North precinct waiting.

All around people jostled past her on their way to and from work. They were like a wave coursing along the wet sidewalk flowing past a rock in the middle. The rain didn't help her mood which was an odd mixture of despondency, fear and excitement.

This can't be so difficult. You've done it once already, she told herself. Another voice within her said, but that was on a case.

You had an excuse to ask him out.

Worryingly that voice was like a police siren. It cut through all other sounds and echoed around her head like a warning. Yet she remained rooted to the spot. Staring across at the precinct. Many people were entering and probably not to gain shelter from the weather. She worried that each new person to pass through the doors would be the cause of her waiting and waiting.

She tried to focus her thoughts on something happier.

The memory of them dancing was the first thing that came to mind. His touch. The way he said, 'Miss Flynn'. Her breathing became more controlled and the sneering voices in her head melted away as she recalled the night at the Ostrich Club.

She wanted it all and was that such a bad thing? She thought of Agatha. The story of her life, married to a lord who was also a spy and a diplomat had thrilled her, inspired her, even.

She was going to ask him out. What was there to lose? Well, a lot, if he said "no". The voice had returned. You'll lose face. You'll lose that dream you have.

Stop!

Then she saw Captain Francis O'Riordan appear on the steps of the precinct. He had his mackintosh on and he looked as if he was ready to head home after another successful day fighting crime. As ever, there was a cigar clamped to the side of his mouth. He shuffled down the step, rainwater dripping from his hat like a broken pipe.

He turned to his right and headed down the street and then popped into a shop's doorway to take shelter from the rain. He was now directly across the street from Bobbie. She lowered her umbrella lest he see her. O'Riordan stayed there for a minute or two, his eyes flicking back towards the precinct.

It was as if he was waiting for someone.

Bobbie kept one eye on the police captain while another made sure Nolan did not escape her. A few minutes later he appeared in the doorway. He held the door open for a patrolman arriving soaked. They exchanged a few words that made both the detective and the patrolman laugh. Then he quickly went down the steps.

Arriving on the sidewalk, he looked left then right. With a shock, Bobbie realised that O'Riordan was waving to him.

This was a surprise because she strongly suspected that Detective Nolan could not abide him. The feeling was probably mutual. A feeling of unease pricked her skin as she watched the young detective head towards the doorway of the shop. This feeling was not only based on the fear that he would see her.

Why was he going to meet O'Riordan like this?

He was now standing in the doorway with the captain. They stood back from the sidewalk and chatted for a moment. It was O'Riordan who was speaking and jabbing his finger. At least, this was something. If they were arguing then Bobbie felt better about their odd meeting.

This feeling barely lasted a minute.

O'Riordan reached inside his pocket and took out a brown envelope. He opened it briefly and to Bobbie's horror, she saw that it was stuffed full of dollars.

Don't, thought Bobbie. Please don't.

Nolan looked around him to the street. It was a furtive look. He was checking who might be around. He took his time and twice Bobbie had to lower her umbrella. Then, from under the rim she saw Nolan's hand grasp the envelope and stuff it in the pocket of his mackintosh.

Bobbie gasped in horror.

There was no question as to what she had just seen. It felt as if her world had come crashing around her. She could barely breathe with the shock of what she'd witnessed. All at once she could feel the dampness of her shoes.

Bobbie turned away immediately and began to walk against the crowd of office workers surging towards her. They banged into her, cursed her, but she didn't care. She walked ahead and didn't know where she was headed and didn't care either.

Something had just ended for her and she felt cold, alone and disillusioned.

The tears came and went and soon were replaced by anger. If that was what he was, a policeman on the take then she had escaped an unimaginable fate. This made her feel better, if only marginally. Then she knew what she had to do.

She needed to go home.

The End

One in ten people leave any kind of rating or review for books they have read on Amazon. Reviews help independent authors, like me, enormously. They act as a pull for other readers (assuming it's a good one!!) - **please consider leaving a review. Thanks for reading!!**

Research Notes

This is a work of fiction. However, it references real-life individuals. Gore Vidal, in his introduction to Lincoln, writes that placing history in fiction or fiction in history has been unfashionable since Tolstoy and that the result can be accused of being neither. He defends the practice, pointing out that writers from Aeschylus to Shakespeare to Tolstoy have done so with, not inconsiderable, success and merit.

I have mentioned a number of key real-life individuals and events in this novel. My intention, in the following section, is to explain a little more about their connection to this period and this story.

Irving Berlin (1888 – 1989)
Irving Berlin was, probably, the most famous, and certainly the most successful, song writer of the early twentieth century.

His break into music came in 1909 when he presented a lyric to a music publisher about Dorando, the Italian marathon runner who had been helped over the line at the 1908 Olympics. The publisher asked did he have music to accompany the lyric. Berlin said "yes" even if his skills on the piano were confined to picking out a tune with one finger.

He became one of the first, and only, songwriters in Tin Pan Alley to write both music and lyrics.

The list of his achievements in song would require a separate book. Suffice to say he has written the best-selling song of all time – *White Christmas*. To this, one may add – *Cheek to Cheek, Top Hat, Putttin' on the Ritz* and his first big hit, *Alexander's Ragtime Band*.

As musical tastes changed, he changed too. He was able to straddle the evolution of the musical on Broadway from a show with a lot of songs unrelated to plot or character to one where the songs were integrated and became an essential part of moving the plot forward.

Annie Get Your Gun was a stage show written in a matter of weeks and spawned a number of new standards of which the most famous are – *Anything You Can Do (I can do Better)* and the ultimate stage song, *There's No Business Like Show business*.

The word 'genius' is overused these days, but I think we're pretty safe here in making this call for Irving Berlin…

Leo Feist (1869 – 1930)

Leopold Feist founded and ran the music publishing firm that bore his name. From the 1920s, at the height of the golden age of popular music, his firm was among the largest publishers of popular music in the world. Their biggest hit was *My Blue Heaven* by Walter Donaldson and George Whitling. The company used the motto "You can't go wrong, with any FEIST Song".

Nelly Bly (1864 – 1922)

Elizabeth Cochran was better known by her pen name Nellie Bly. In an astonishing career, she created the concept of investigative journalism with her daring undercover stint in a mental institution which uncovered the abuses being experienced by women. The expose was made at great risk to her personal safety as she feigned insanity to gain admission to an asylum. She spent ten days committed and witnessed first-hand the brutality and neglect that was commonplace in such institutions. Her book, *Ten Days in a Mad-House*, was a sensation which prompted the asylum to implement reforms and cemented her fame.

Later in her career she made a record-breaking trip around the world in 72 days to emulate Phileas Fogg the fictional hero of Jules Verne's *Around the World in Eighty Days*. She accomplished this journey for the most part on her own, which, given the risks involved, was as remarkable as the speed with which she managed the 25,000-mile journey.

Tin Pan Alley

Whether or not the story of how Tin Pan Alley gained its name is true, there is no question that it was the centre of music publishing between the 1920's and the 1950's. The location of Tin Pan Alley changed over the years with the arrival of new theatres on or near Broadway. It began in the area between 28th street and 6th Avenue ending up in the area between 42nd and 50th streets.

The great music publishers of the day were situated there, Leo Feist, Charles Harris, T.B. Harms & Francis, Day & Hunter, Inc., Shapiro, Bernstein & Co., Inc., Waterson, Berlin & Snyder, Inc., and M. Witmark & Sons, Inc. They represented the great songwriters who arrived to make their name in New York: Irving Berlin, Jerome Kern, PG Wodehouse, George & Ira Gershwin, Lorenz Hart, Richard Rogers, Oscar Hammerstein – the list is endless, their songs will live forever.

About the Author

Jack Murray was born in Northern Ireland but has spent over half his life living just outside London, except for some periods spent in Australia, Monte Carlo, and the US.

An artist, as well as a writer, Jack's work features in collections around the world and he has exhibited in Britain, Ireland, and Monte Carlo.

A spin off series from the Kit Aston novels was published in 2020 featuring Aunt Agatha as a young woman solving mysterious murders.

Another spin off series is features Inspector Jellicoe. It is set in the late 1950's/early 1960's.

Jack finished work on a World War II trilogy in 2022. The three books look at the war from both the British and the German side. They have been published through Lume Books and are available on Amazon.